BORN INTO DESTINY

A Forsaken Sinners MC Novella

By Shelly Morgan

BORN INTO DESTINY

Limitless Publishing, LLC
Kailua, HI 96734
www.limitlesspublishing.com

Formatting: Limitless Publishing

ISBN-13:978-1-68058-583-4
ISBN-10:1-68058-583-5

DEDICATION

This book is dedicated to my children: Marcus, Mikayla, and Owen. You are more than just my children, you are the reason I wake up in the morning, the reason I strive to be a better person, and the light of my life. I love you three more than you could ever know.

CHAPTER 1

19 Weeks Pregnant

Dani

Making my way out to my truck, I stuff my phone in my purse, ignoring the incoming call from Zane.

Today is my doctor's appointment to not only make sure my ribs are healing from the altercation with Sara's psychotic ex a few weeks ago, but also to get our first ultrasound of the baby. They did a quick ultrasound when I was in the hospital with the bruised ribs, but at that time, they were only looking to make sure the baby hadn't been harmed. Thank fuck there was nothing wrong with the baby or else I would have brought that fucker Rick back to life just to kill him again myself.

We weren't able to really get a good look at the baby then, so I'm excited about today. I can't wait to see how the baby has grown and to just see him or her. We could find out the sex if we wanted to, but I told Zane I wanted to wait until the baby was born

1

and have it be a surprise. Zane said he couldn't wait; he needed to know if we were having a boy or girl so he could better prepare. Not sure how he's going to prepare differently if we have a girl instead of a boy, or vice versa, but what-the-fuck-ever.

However, Zane sent me a text five minutes ago saying he isn't going to be able to make it to the appointment. He's caught up with club business or some shit like that. He then informed me that he was going to send Toby or Louie to pick me up and "accompany" me to my appointment. He doesn't think I can drive myself, like the moment he impregnated me I need someone to help me do the most basic of tasks. He thinks I'm glass and will break. I swear, one of these days I'm going to knock that fucker upside his head for the shit he says. I know he means well, at least most of the time he does, but I'm stronger than he thinks. He needs a sensor most days. That mouth of his gets him in so much trouble, and not just with me, but with some of the brothers too.

As I close the door, I hear my phone ring again. When I look at the screen, I see that it's Louie. I better answer before he brings the whole damn club down on my ass. "Whatever Zane told you, just forget it. I'm already on my way and I don't need a babysitter or someone to wipe my junk after pissing in a cup for the good ol' doctor."

I can hear Louie choking on something on the other end. "Fuck, Dani! Did you really have to put that image in my head? Shit!"

Not really in the mood for small talk, I wait him out. "Okay, I won't go with you, but when Blaze finds out you know he's gonna be pissed."

That makes me laugh. "He won't be the only one pissed. Why don't you let me deal with Zane? He ain't nothing I can't handle." Hanging up the phone, I turn it off and make the ten minute drive to the clinic.

***

I've barely taken a seat in the waiting room when I hear the nurse call my name. Once in the room, she takes all my vitals and has me pee in the cup. I hate that fucking part; makes me feel all gross and shit. It's disgusting to think that someone is in a lab somewhere, or even sitting at one of those desks in the hall that I passed on my way back here, looking at my piss or whatever it is they do. Fucking gross.

Once I'm done with that, she has me change into one of those paper gowns. You know, the ones that tie in the front and barely cover anything? They are fucking pointless if you ask me. Might as well have me sitting here buck ass naked. I'd probably be more comfortable that way too.

Not even a minute after I get resituated on the exam table, Dr. Carmichael, my OBGYN, knocks on the door. I'm glad she doesn't keep me waiting long. I've heard that some people have had to sit here in these paper gowns for up to a half an hour. *Fuck that shit.* I'd just fucking leave—or maybe open the door and tell someone they better get their ass in here before I start throwing shit. Yeah, that probably wouldn't be a good idea, but what do they expect? My temper wasn't very good *before* I got pregnant. What can I say, I get irritated and pissed easily. Now,

3

though? Yeah, if you even sneeze weird or look at me wrong, I'm gonna be on your ass. I'm not proud of this, but it is what it is.

"Hello, Danielle. How are you feeling today?" Dr. Carmichael asks as she closes the door.

"Dani, please. Call me Dani. And I'm doing okay, though I think others would tell you differently." I laugh because I can just hear it now—Zane would probably ask to speak to the good doctor privately to see if there was something she could do about my mood swings. Tough luck, fucker.

She walks over to a chair by the desk and flips through my file. "The urine sample you left came back fine, and your vitals are looking good. Let's measure your stomach quick, we'll take a look at your ribs to make sure they are healing okay, then the ultrasound tech will come in." I nod my head and lie back gently on the exam table, being careful of my bruised ribs. They're a lot better than even a few days ago, but are still sore when I move a certain way.

She pulls the gown up but leaves the sheet I have over my legs, covering my goodies down below.

Dr. Carmichael takes out a small tape measure and places it on my stomach. I've just recently started noticing the difference in my growing tummy. "You're measuring at about twenty centimeters, which is good." Putting the tape measure away, she then starts poking around on my ribs. I try to hold back my wince, but she sees it.

"Still a little tender?" she asks. I nod and try to hide my eye roll, but come on; of course they're still fucking tender! That shit takes weeks to fucking heal, and even then, I've heard people still feel pain every

4

now and then.

When she's done with her assessment, she helps me sit up and to pull the gown down. "Why don't you get dressed so you're more comfortable? I'll be back in a couple of minutes with the tech, then we can take a look at your little one." I smile and nod, thankful I can put my clothes back on.

It takes me a little longer than usual to get dressed again since my ribs are screaming at me. Just as I'm pulling down my shirt, there's a knock on the door before Dr. Carmichael and a younger guy rolling a machine behind him come walking into the room.

"Dani, this is Justin. He'll be the one doing the ultrasound today," Dr. Carmichael says.

Justin holds out his hand for me to shake which I take before he sits down in front of the ultrasound machine.

"Why don't you lay down and make yourself as comfortable as possible?" Justin says as he motions me back over to the table I was on just minutes before.

Dr. Carmichael again helps me lie down, then pushes up my shirt enough for Justin to have access to my stomach for the ultrasound.

"Can we pull these down just a bit? I'll tuck a towel in there too so your pants don't get goo on them." I don't answer, I just roll my pants down farther so he has access to what he needs.

He squirts cold jelly on my stomach, which makes me jump a bit, then he starts moving that wand thingy around on my stomach. I look to the screen, trying to make sense of what I'm seeing, but really, I have no idea. It all looks like a bunch of nothing to me.

A few seconds pass, then I hear this loud whooshing sound. It never fails to amaze me every time I get to hear my baby's heartbeat.

"The heartbeat sounds good and strong." He doesn't look at me when he speaks; he's too busy looking at the screen and typing away on the keyboard.

As he moves the wand around, he points out parts of the baby that I can barely make out.

Finally, Justin looks at me. "Would you like to know what you're having?"

Without moving my gaze from the screen, I answer, "No. I want it to be a surprise."

He doesn't question me and neither does Dr. Carmichael. I'm sure she's wondering what Zane is going to say because he has been very vocal during our past appointments about wanting to know the sex, but if he wanted to know, he should have worked harder to make it to the appointment.

They finally get everything they need and hand me a towel to clean the goo off my stomach. When I sit up, Justin hands me some pictures he must have printed out without me even realizing. "Baby's first picture," he says with a smile in his voice, but I don't look to confirm. I'm too consumed looking at the pictures of my baby.

I barely remember the walk out of the room or to my car. I don't even think I stopped to schedule my next appointment. I can't get enough of looking at my little guy. Yes, I said little guy. Don't ask me how, but I just know that I'm having a boy. I'm going to have a son, I can feel it. Maybe it's in my DNA or maybe destiny is throwing me a bone, I don't know. What I *do* know is that when I found out I was pregnant, I pictured this little boy with my dark hair and Zane's eyes.

CHAPTER 2

22 Weeks Pregnant

Zane

I wake to the sound of crashing pans and plates coming from the kitchen. I slept on the couch last night because Dani kicked me out of our bed again. Seems like it's becoming a regular occurrence lately. She says I'm being a jackass, but really, she's the one who is being unreasonable and a bitch. All I'm trying to do is make sure that she's safe and taken care of when I can't be around, which happens to be a lot lately.

It probably doesn't help that she's still pissed at me from a couple of weeks ago. I couldn't make it to her doctor's appointment. I did everything in my fucking power, I even knocked a couple of the brothers' heads together to make it back on time, but it just didn't happen. Then, when I finally got home, I asked her what she found out: were we having a boy or a girl? She told me she didn't find out, said that she wanted to be surprised. I got pissed because I thought we had decided we would find out.

I know she wants to be surprised, but when we last discussed it I thought we said we'd find out. But she said that since I wasn't there, I didn't have a say in it. What-the-fuck-ever, I guess. If it ain't one thing, it's another with her.

If things at home aren't bad enough lately, now things with the club are heating up too. From what I've heard since transferring here from our Texas charter, we haven't had any real threats against the club for about a decade. We haven't had any club wars, problems with territories, or club rivals. But we've heard of a new club moving in the next town over, and from the stories we hear, they aren't very respectable. It doesn't even sound like they're even in a club for brotherhood; they only want power and to scare and control people.

We've decided to keep our eyes on them and have been doing some light surveillance. So far, though, they've kept a pretty low profile. Maybe because they know we're close and don't want to start anything until they have their base set up. Who knows?

Mack has me helping out a lot since I did mostly surveillance and security in the Marines, so this is cake to me. I told him I can't keep doing this with the baby on the way, but he has promised me Dani is fine and has a tail on her without her knowing to make sure nothing happens. I gave him six weeks then I'm done being away from her for longer than a couple hours at a time, and definitely not being more than a twenty minute ride away. He hopes we'll have a good handle on this situation by then, though, and so do I. I don't need a club war starting when I'm trying to prepare for fatherhood.

Getting up, I make my way into the kitchen. I see Dani in one of my t-shirts that hits her mid-thigh, throwing what looks like a smoking pan into the sink, cussing the whole time about stupid fucking eggs and shitty fucking bacon.

My laugh draws her attention to me. I should stop myself, knowing it will just piss her off more, but I can't help myself. She's so fucking sexy when she's angry. "Need some help, Baby Girl?" I ask when I finally calm down enough to speak.

She's glaring, not answering me, so I walk up to her and take her lips with mine. She hesitates at first, tries to push me away, but she kisses me back after I kiss her harder, not letting her push me away. "Mmm, fuck breakfast. I'll just eat you," I groan into her mouth before I lift her up and place her on the counter.

Spreading her legs, my hand travels up her inner thigh. When I encounter no resistance, I growl my approval of her not wearing panties, then kneel down and give her a long, hard lick up her center.

"Holy shit! Yes, right there. Don't stop. Don't you *dare* fucking stop," she breathes out as I continue to flick my tongue over her clit. Shit, she tastes so fucking good. Better than any food I've ever had.

It only takes me a solid minute before she's withering on the counter, hanging onto my hair for dear life, and screaming out my name as she falls over the cliff of ecstasy.

Standing up, I pull her shirt up with me as I go, and toss it somewhere behind me, not even caring where it lands.

When I'm standing between her legs, I push my sweatpants down my hips and say, "My turn," then I kiss her roughly as I push my cock inside her tight pussy in one thrust.

I pause for a second to give her time to catch her breath, but I can't wait longer before I need to move. "Sorry, Baby Girl, you just feel so fucking good," I mutter into her neck. I think since she's become pregnant, her sweet pussy has gotten even tighter, if that's possible.

Dani starts clawing at my arms, pulling me closer as her lips search for mine. Not being able to deny her anything, I give her what she wants.

As soon as our lips meet, I start thrusting faster, deeper, harder. This makes her scream, but I silence her with my mouth, grabbing the back of her neck so she can't get away. I thrust in three more times before I go stiff, spilling my seed inside her.

We stay connected, neither of us having the energy to move. That is, until I smell smoke seconds before the fire alarm goes off.

Pulling out of her heat a little too fast, she starts to fall forward, but I catch her, making sure she's steady before turning around to see what's on fire. That's when I notice the shirt I practically ripped off of Dani and threw behind me is now lying on the stovetop, a burning mess, smoke filling the kitchen. "Shit," I yell, racing over to the drawer and pulling out a pair of tongs. How the fuck did we not notice this?

I try to grab the burning shirt with the tongs, but every time I think I have a good hold on it, it breaks apart and falls before I can get it to the sink. "Shit!

Fuck!" I curse.

Suddenly, I feel wetness hit me in the back of the head and a stream of water moving from my head to the shirt that is now on the counter beside the stove, still on fire. "What the fuck?" I say, turning toward the stream of water.

Dani is holding the sprayer from the sink, drenching the burning shirt until the fire is out. But instead of releasing the trigger to stop the flow of water, she moves it back toward me, hitting me in the face. I'm stunned at first, not believing she's actually having a water fight with me inside, but her laughter breaks me out of my shock. "Baby Girl, I suggest you run," I say before I take off in the direction she's in.

She screams as she dashes out of the kitchen, trying to run up the stairs to get away from me, but I catch her on the first step. "Where do you think you're going, huh?" I growl, then lift her up and start carrying her up the stairs. But before we even make it up two steps, my phone starts to ring.

"You're not gonna answer that, are you?" Dani asks, seeming almost desperate and vulnerable. I hate to upset her, but it could be club shit. "I'm sorry, Baby Girl. But it's Mack and could be important," I say, hoping she understands. I know that she gets the club is important and sometimes has to come first, but she has to know that she will always be my number one priority.

"Whatever. I'll be upstairs getting ready for work," she says, but she doesn't sound angry, just sad.

"I'm sorry," I whisper as she walks up the stairs, but she doesn't answer. Either she didn't hear me or just doesn't reply.

CHAPTER 3

24 Weeks Pregnant

Dani

Things with Zane seem to go from bad to worse, then get better and are amazing, before plummeting back down. I feel like I get brought up so high, like I'm floating near heaven, and then I'm knocked down and buried in Hell where everything hurts in the most painful of ways; every word, every look, every touch. I've tried talking to him about it, tell him what I've been feeling, but he just doesn't understand.

When I first found out I was pregnant, I was scared, and frankly a little upset that I was going to have a baby without planning for it. Was I going to be a good mother? Sure, I had my grandmother as a role model, but my mother died when I was so young. What if I'm horrible at the parenting thing? What if I'm not ready to be a mother? What if after I have this baby, I don't want it? I know that's a horrible thought, but it's crossed my mind. I never really thought about having children before. I was content with just living my life on the edge, doing what I want and having fun in the process. Never had I thought I'd become a mother.

After it finally sank in, I couldn't think of a life without my baby anymore, but that doesn't mean that I'm ready or not scared. And with Zane gone a lot, my fears have seemed to intensify and I find myself thinking things I shouldn't. Like, is raising a child around a motorcycle club a good idea? But then I think of everything I've been through and what Mack and everyone else in the club mean to me and I know that right or wrong, I wouldn't do it any other way.

Then I think about leaving the shop, handing the reins over to Louie, so I can be at home with the baby. But then I can't see myself not doing what I love. So should I bring the baby to work with me, or will Zane and I have to work out our schedules so one of us will always be at home? With the way things have been lately and him never being around, would he even be home at all to help me with the baby? If not, I would either have to stop working or hire babysitter. And that brings thoughts of if I could really trust someone with my baby that I don't know that well and that would be outside of the club.

I just can't catch a fucking break. I'm exhausted because I haven't been sleeping at night. I can't get comfortable most nights, and then the nights that Zane is gone I stay up worrying about him, wondering where he is. There have been some nights that I just couldn't sleep, so I've called Mack to see if he heard anything from him, but a couple of times, Mack said that Zane wasn't on a job. That had confused me at first, but I just passed it off as wires getting crossed. Maybe Zane told me where he was but I forgot, but after the third time, I started wondering if he was sneaking around on me. I'm not saying he could be cheating, but what is he doing if he's not on club business and not home? And why wouldn't Mack at least know something? I think after the last time, Mack was even starting to get suspicious of what he was doing. Not wanting to cause problems between them, I decided not to call him anymore when Zane wasn't home at night anymore.

He does come home eventually, it's just usually around three or four in the morning. He doesn't seem like he's hiding anything, but I usually pretend to be sleeping too when he climbs into bed. Maybe next time I should try talking to him about it, but then I remember how strained things are between us and figure it probably won't turn out well so what's the point? Either he's going to tell me something I won't like, he'll say it's nothing when I know it's something, or maybe he'll brush it off completely, who knows? It probably won't make me feel better, so for the baby's sake, I'm trying not to think about it, but it's hard.

After I get dressed, I make my way to my truck to head into the shop. Sara wanted to talk to me about a tattoo idea she had. It's her first tattoo and I'm honored she wants me to do it. I thought since she and Louie have been getting a lot closer lately that maybe she'd have him do it. No matter, whether I do it or he does, I know she'll be in good hands. Though, I'm sure Toby would want me to do it. He knows Louie doesn't feel anything besides friendship toward Sara, but I think just the idea of any man's hands on his woman gets his pulse racing. It's the same thing with any of the brothers; whether it's their old lady or plaything of the week, they don't want to see anyone's hands on her but their own.

When I make it into the shop, Sara is already there waiting for me, talking with Louie. "Hey, girl! How are you?" she asks me when I walk in the door.

I smile and give her a hug. "I'm good, babe. How are things with you?" It seems like forever since I've last seen her, but I know it's only been a couple of days. Even though we talk on the phone almost daily, I still miss seeing her every day like I used to. She's still working for me, but she's taken some time off for herself after her ex tried to take her. Then Toby proposed soon after we both got out of the hospital. I wasn't surprised one bit when they told us the news. I always knew Toby was the marrying type once he found the right woman. And they are so perfect together, I couldn't be happier. I just hope they wait till after I have the baby. I don't want to be fat and uncomfortable during the ceremony and party afterward.

"So tell me about your idea. What do you want done?" I ask as we start walking toward my station. When I sit down, I take out my sketch pad, hoping that she'll let me free hand it, whatever it is she wants.

"Well, actually, I have two things I want," she says almost shyly. Hm, that's interesting. What could she possibly want that would have her embarrassed?

"Okay…" I say, waiting for her to continue.

She's looking down at her lap and bouncing her leg up and down, so I reach my hand over to calm her, give her my reassurance. "Hey, whatever it is, we'll do it. If it's what you really want, I'll make it happen. Just talk to me so I know what I'm dealing with," I say in a soothing tone.

When she looks up at me, it's with resolve. Good girl. "Well, the first one is a fighting angel. I want you to design it and I want it on my back." That's kind of surprising. Usually for a first tattoo, you'd start off with something a little smaller than a full back piece, but we can work it in several sessions if need be.

"All right, I can do that. Anything specific you want in it or just something like an avenging angel?" I ask, jotting down notes so I can start sketching later. I already have an idea forming, but I need to know what she wants before I start.

"Nothing specific really, but I thought maybe the angel could be holding a sword or dagger?" she asks, not really unsure about what she's saying, more like asking what I think.

"Yeah, that's actually what I was thinking. I have an idea in my head. Let me draw it out and I can show you in a couple of days. Then we can discuss if it's in the direction you are thinking and we'll go from there. That work?" Hopefully this isn't something she wants today because I hate rushing on pieces like this.

"Yeah, that would be perfect. Whenever you're done," she says with a smile.

"Okay, great! Now what about the other idea?" I ask after making notes about the angel.

"I want a brand," she says bluntly. I look up at her and see that she's serious.

"A brand?" I ask, not really sure what she's asking for. I think I know what she's talking about, but want

17

to be sure.

"I want everyone to know that I'm Toby's girl and that he's mine. I've heard of some old ladies doing it and I want to do it too." I've heard of people getting one, I guess I just never saw it being necessary. I mean, you wear his cut and property patch, sure, but a tattoo? Maybe I'm old-fashioned, but I just think having a man's name tattooed on your skin is bad luck, like you're jinxing it.

"Are you sure?" I ask, just needing to hear her say it. I'd hate to ink something on her skin that is permanent, then have her regret it.

"Yes, I'm sure. I've thought long and hard about this and it's what I want. I talked to Toby and he asked the same thing, but when I told him how much I wanted it, he said that he'd be okay with it. Said he might even do the same thing." She laughs at that last part. I laugh too, imagining Toby getting a brand. Most men won't brand themselves to a woman, thinking it should only be the other way around. But if anyone would do it, it would be Toby.

"Well, I can design one for him based off of yours if you want," I add when we're done laughing.

She looks at me hopefully. "You could do that? You could make his look like mine, but not feminine? I want mine to have a feminine touch," she says, talking fast, an excited glint in her eye now that it's more real to her.

"Of course I can do it. I can do anything you want, girl, you should know that by now," I say seriously, but then smile so she knows I'm not mad. "Let me work on these and I'll get them to you in a couple of days." She hugs me before walking out of the shop, and I get right to work. I'm actually really excited about doing both of these for her. I think she's really gonna like what I have in mind. It's going to be kickass, but feminine. It'll be perfect for her.

CHAPTER 4

26 Weeks Pregnant

Zane

I'm fucking exhausted. Mack has been running me ragged with surveillance on that club that moved in practically next door, The Street Kings. So far, they haven't made any suspicious moves that would necessitate their removal. But Mack isn't satisfied, says that there's something there, he can feel it. I told him I'm done in two weeks, that I can't keep doing this. I know Dani must be pissed, but after the first couple of weeks of yelling and fighting, now she's just distant. I fucking hate it. I hate that I'm not home. I hate that I can't tell her what's really going on. I just want to be home with her, hold her in my arms, and enjoy this pregnancy with her.

On top of that, I was contacted by her father. I have no idea how he found us, but he wants a sit-down with Dani. I'm not having that shit, but he won't give it up. I've been doing extra surveillance on his ass to make sure he stays in line and doesn't try to approach her. Maybe I should just bring it to the table and let the club deal with it. Dani is one of us, a part of this club, so it's only right that we vote on what should happen. We can give him an ultimatum or scare the shit out of him to make him stay away.

When Dani's grandmother died, I know he showed up at the funeral, and Dani was pissed. She told him to leave her alone and not contact her again, so I'm trying to keep him away. I don't want her to know that he's around and wanting to meet with her. She doesn't need the added stress with her being pregnant.

I walk into the club and see Mack come out of his office. When he sees me, he points at me with a pissed off look on his face. "You. My office. *Now,*" he says before turning back around and heading into his office. Great, just fucking great. I don't need this shit right now!

Sighing, I follow him, knowing I can't say no. I just hope we can make this quick. I want to tell him what I found out about The Street Kings, which is absolutely fucking nothing, and get home to my girl.

I close the door, not making a move to sit down, but Mack isn't having that. "Sit the fuck down. Me and you need to have a talk," his voice booms.

I stare at him for a second before I take a seat. "What is it, Mack? I just want to go home to my girl," I say, rubbing my eyes.

"Oh yeah? You actually going home this time or you got somewhere more fucking important you need to be?" he asks with a sneer. What the hell is he going on about?

"Why don't you just spit out whatever the fuck it is

you're getting at, Mack, 'cause I'm too fucking tired to read between the lines," I say, looking directly into his eyes, not backing down.

He leans forward and points at me. "I'm talking about you telling your *girl* that you're on club business when you're not. So my question is: where the fuck have you been off to when you're not here and not at home?" I stare at him blankly, trying to figure out what I should say. I know exactly what he's talking about, but I'm not sure if I'm ready to bring the club in on this shit with Dani's father.

Mack must see me contemplating telling him because he scoffs, "Out with it, boy!"

Sighing, I give in. "It's not what you're probably thinking. I fucking love Dani more than anything. I would never do anything to hurt her or fuck things up with her. That's why I haven't said anything to her about where I've been and I wasn't ready to bring it to the club, but it's probably time since I haven't been able to resolve it myself. Frankly, I'm just fucking tired of it." I pause for a beat, looking at him to make sure he's with me and not letting his anger and assumptions cloud what I'm saying.

When I know he's still with me and see that he's actually calmed down a bit, I continue. "Dani's father contacted me. He's here and he wants to see her. I've been trying to get him to fuck off, but he's not having it. I've done everything except threaten death, but he's not budging. Said it's his right to see her and he needs to talk to her about something important, though he won't say what." I leave it at that, because that's all I really know. With looking for shit on the other club Mack has me watching, I haven't really been able to

22

dig deep into Dani's father.

Mack is quiet for a couple of minutes, probably trying to digest what I just said, and come up with the best way to handle it. Thank fuck for that because I'm out of ideas. Short of killing the fucker, what else can we do besides just keep an eye on him and make sure he doesn't come near her?

Finally, Mack speaks. "Maybe we should set up a meet. You, me, and him. He can either tell us what it's about and we can decide if we need to bring Dani in on it or he keeps quiet and we push him out by any means necessary." I nod my head, willing to agree to anything at this point if it means we can deal with it without Dani finding out. It feels good to have at least Mack on my side. I'm not sure how he found out about me not being home, but I can only assume Dani called him. I wish I could give her something, but right now, I think it's best to keep her in the dark.

"Do you know how to contact him?" Mack asks. I pull out my phone and write down the number I got for him. Hopefully it's still his number; my information might be old.

Mack pulls out his phone, dials the number, and then puts it on speakerphone before laying it on the desk between us. We listen to the phone ring twice, then someone answers, and I know it's who we want by his greeting. "Hello, Dani?" her father says through the phone.

"This isn't Dani, but we're the only ones you're talking to until we know what you want with her," Mack says into the phone.

It's quiet for a couple of moments, then her father speaks. "Who is this?" he asks, sounding annoyed.

"My name is Mack. And Blaze is here as well, though you probably know him as Zane. What should I call you?" We wait for his response. I never even asked for his name and I don't think Dani has ever mentioned it.

"My name is Daniel," he finally says. How fucking original. Dani must have been named after her dad. Does she know that? I don't think she'd call herself Dani if she did, though, it's not like Danielle is any better.

"All right, Daniel. This is what's gonna happen. We'll send you a date, time, and location for you to meet us and you're going to tell us what it is that's so important that you need to speak to our girl. If we decide it's something we need to bring her in on, we'll set up a meet on our terms. You either take it or leave it, but if you decide not to meet us, we expect you to leave California and never try to contact her again or we will have problems. You feel me?" Mack threatens in a cold, calculating voice. If I didn't know him or have him on my side, I would be frightened. Mack isn't someone you fuck with, that's for sure. Hopefully Daniel heeds the warning clear in his voice.

The line is silent for so long, I worry that he's hung up, but then he answers, "We need to meet soon."

"Just wait for our fucking word. Be where we tell you, when we tell you, or you leave and we better not hear or see you around again." Mack doesn't wait for him to reply, just hangs up the phone and looks at me. "Go home, son. Get some sleep. Hopefully tomorrow we'll have this shit figured out." I stand and slap his back then head out the door, eager to get home to my girl.

CHAPTER 5

28 Weeks Pregnant

Dani

I feel so fucking fat! I know that's probably cliché for a pregnant chick, but it's the goddamn truth. And my back hurts, my feet are swollen, and I'm so fucking tired! All the time! I can't catch a fucking break. The only good thing I can say that has happened in the last week is that Zane has been home more and I don't feel as worried anymore, though I get the feeling he's still hiding something.

I tried to bring up those weeks he wasn't home and told him about the times I called Mack, but he said it was nothing to be concerned with, just a problem that arose, but now he and Mack are dealing with it. Knowing that Mack is involved, at least now, makes me feel a little bit better, but not by much. He's still keeping something from me, but I suppose it probably has something to do with the club. I know he'd tell me if it had something to do with me.

Today Sara is coming in to finish her angel tattoo and we're going to try and get her brand done as well. That one isn't so big and it's on her forearm, so it shouldn't be a problem. She's done really well with the back tattoo for it being her first. We've only had to schedule two sessions, when I thought it would at least take three, maybe four.

She's absolutely in love with the design I came up with for her back, so much so that she even cried. Then when I showed her what I had planned for her brand and that I had one made up for Toby already too, she cried some more. If I didn't know better, I'd think she was pregnant too. Bitch has been crying as much as me lately. But I'm so happy that she likes what I came up with.

It took some work, but I was able to get everything she wanted into the designs. The angel is kneeling on one knee, with his arms resting on a sword in front of him. His head is down, but you can tell he's fierce with just the way his stance is. She was shocked when I showed it to her, thinking the angel was going to be female, but I thought it was fitting to give her a male guardian angel, kind of like Toby. He was my inspiration of course when designing it.

Then her brand is pretty simple and straight forward. It's the MC's emblem, with a little feminine flair, then it says 'Property of Toby' at the bottom. I think it's pretty fucking cool. I'd put the same thing on myself, minus the Toby part, of course, if I was into that sort of thing. I think the only thing I would be willing to do is get the MC's emblem, but no names. Then the one I made for Toby would be an extension of his current club tat. He already has the emblem and club name, so if he approves, I'll just add at the bottom 'Doll's Old Man.' I'm not sure if he's actually going to do it or not, but I look forward to the look on his face when he sees it; it should be a good laugh either way.

When I walk into the shop, I notice Toby first, then Sara. She's coming in from the back and Louie is tailing her. "Hey, guys. Sara, you ready?" I ask as I walk up to them, hugging first Toby, then Louie, before pulling Sara in for a hug. It's awkward hugging the guys since they're so tall and muscular, and I'm just fucking huge with my belly hanging out in front of me. Seriously, this kid is gonna come out weighing a ton if I keep tacking on weight like I have been. The doctors say that it's not all baby, which doesn't make me feel better, but I've already told Toby to be ready for me it the time comes to help me get back into shape. I know I can still whoop his ass.

"Yup, all set. I've already got everything ready for you," Sara says as she follows me toward my station.

Toby walks in behind us, the excitement in his eyes I'm sure is because his woman is branding herself to him today.

We're able to finish her back piece in just under two hours. I suggest we take a break for lunch, which thankfully Sara agrees to, then we'll start on her other tat.

When I walk into the break room, I see that Zane is there, unpacking what looks like take-out from the Chinese place down the street. "Oh my God, that smells so fucking good!" I say as I inhale the sweet aroma of all the food he's laying out in front of me.

I take a seat and don't wait for anyone else before I

start dishing huge portions of vegetable fried rice, sweet and sour chicken, and four egg rolls. Don't judge me!

Zane laughs before sitting down beside me, kissing my cheek.

"I hope you have more bags hidden somewhere, 'cause I'm not sharin'," I say with a mouthful of food. I hear Sara and Toby chuckle, but don't pay them any attention.

"Don't worry, Baby Girl, this is all for you," Zane says with a sweet smile on his face. Goddamn I love this man, he's so good to me.

When I finish eating, we all head back to my station. I'm surprised that both Zane and Toby are sitting down watching. Well, I guess Toby isn't really a surprise, but Zane is. I wonder why he hasn't left yet. I thought for sure he'd be doing club business since I'm busy here.

I place the stencil on Sara's arm, then I get to work.

Zane comes over when I'm halfway done with the tattoo and looks at my work. "That's awesome, Baby Girl. Are you having Louie do yours next?" he asks in a serious voice. I look up at him, trying to gauge if he's really being serious or not, but I can't find a hint of sarcasm.

"Uh, no. I'm not branding myself," I say as I look down and get back to work.

Zane doesn't say anything for a while, so I look up at him to see if he's even still standing there. He is, and he doesn't look happy. "And why the fuck not? You're my Old Lady, aren't ya? You're having my baby. Why the fuck wouldn't you want to wear my brand?"

I'm pissed instantly just from his tone of voice. He's never mentioned it before and he has no fucking reason to get pissed at me now, all because I don't want a fucking brand with his name on it. "Yes, I'm your Old Lady and yes, I'm having your fucking baby, but that doesn't mean I'm going to get a brand," I say, staring at him head-on, not willing to back down on this. He needs to fucking understand this; just because we're together, we love each other, and are having a baby, does not fucking mean I have to tattoo his name on my body.

"Sara's getting one to show her man love, respect, and loyalty by branding herself. Why the hell won't you? Huh?" Is he serious right now?

Standing up, I get right in his face. "What are you trying to say, Blaze? That I don't love you or this club? That I don't respect you or this club? That I'm not fucking loyal to you or the club? Huh? Is that what you're fucking saying to me right now?" I yell, no longer able to hold my own temper in.

He must realize what he just said because he looks down and when he looks back up, he has a look of anguish and regret on his face. Good, asshole. I hope you fucking feel like shit now. How could he even fucking say something like that to me?

"That's not what I meant, Baby Girl. I was just upset that you don't want to wear my brand," he says softly, but I just can't fucking get over what he said. It cut me deep. He and this club mean more to me than my own life. I would do anything for Zane or anyone that's a part of the MC, even lay down my own life. You'd think after everything we've been through, he would know that by now.

"No, you were pissed because one of your brothers one-upped you. You just can't stand the fucking idea that someone has something—" I stop abruptly, suddenly feeling hot and dizzy, unsteady on my feet.

Reaching behind me, I search for something to hold onto, but don't find anything. I feel myself falling, but before I hit the floor, I feel strong arms wrap around me, holding me, preventing me from falling. "Whoa, Baby Girl, you okay?" Zane asks, worried.

I close my eyes to try and stop the world from spinning and nod my head. "Dani, what happened?" I hear Sara say from close by.

"I-I, uh, I don't know. I felt dizzy there for minute, but I'm better now. I don't know what happened," I say as I open my eyes. I still feel hot and a little unsteady, but I don't want them to worry. "I'm fine now," I say as I try to push Zane off of me, my earlier anger coming back, but he won't let me go.

"Dani, stop it. I'm not letting you go, you almost fucking passed out. That's not normal. I think we should take you to the doctor, make sure you and the baby are okay," Zane says. I can tell this has him extremely worried, but it was probably just because I was seriously pissed off.

"I don't need to go to the doctor, I said I'm fine now. It only happened because I was pissed off and all the blood rushed to my head. As soon as you let me go and leave me the fuck alone until I calm down, I'll be fucking fine," I seethe.

Zane looks uncertain, but eventually he cautiously lets me go. "All right, I'll let you calm down, but if you start feeling dizzy again, I'm taking you in," he says while looking at me, then he turns toward Toby. "Keep an eye on her, brother," he says, still sounding upset and a little angry, then he walks out of the room. A couple seconds later I hear the bell over the door jingle, signaling he left the shop.

Turning back around, I say, "Let me just run to the bathroom then we'll finish your ink." I don't wait for either of them to reply, I just walk out of the room and lock myself in the bathroom. I can't believe he said those things to me. Does he really not trust me or think that I don't love him? Does he think that I'm not loyal to him or the club, just because I won't get a brand?

I feel tears start to fall, but I make no move to wipe them away. I'm too crushed and hurt to care.

A quiet knock brings me out of my thoughts. Thinking it's Sara checking on me, I open the door without checking my face, but it's not Sara. It's Zane.

"Oh, Baby Girl, come here. I'm so fucking sorry," he says as he takes me into his arms. Having his arms around me, comforting me, has me losing it completely. I sob into his chest, letting all the anger and pain out. "It's okay, I've got you. I'm sorry. I'm so fucking sorry," he whispers over and over until I'm all cried out.

CHAPTER 6

30 Weeks Pregnant

Zane

I'm on my way to meet up with Mack. We need to figure out what we're going to do about Dani's father. When we met with him that morning, he told us he needed to talk to Dani, but still seemed hesitant to tell us what it was about.

Mack was pissed because he has had nothing to do with her and now he wants to show up like it's his right to talk to her. He even told him that, said that *he* was her father, not him. Daniel was lucky we were even giving him this chance to tell us what was so important instead of throwing his ass to the curb or putting him to ground for leaving Dani after her mother died. I still don't understand how he could do that. I don't care how devastated you are about losing your wife; you should never abandon your child.

Daniel finally told us why he needed to speak with her. He said that her mother had cancer—they'd found out when she was pregnant with Dani. That part I already knew from when we were kids and Dani told me a little about what happened. But her dad went further. He was worried because the doctor who treated her mother said it could be genetic. He wanted to make sure Dani was okay and wanted her to get tested.

At first, I worried that he was right, that we needed to get her in ASAP, with or without her knowledge of why. But Mack told me that the doctors would have noticed it already if she had cancer like her mother. We still want her to be tested, but we don't think it's something that needs to happen right now, and we most certainly don't want to worry or stress her out while she's pregnant—though I may mention it the next time we see her doctor, maybe while Dani is setting up her next appointment.

Now we have to figure out what we're going to do about Daniel. We told him that we would discuss it. He knows she's pregnant, though I have no idea how, and that makes him think it's imperative to get it done right this fucking second. He said he's not leaving until either she gets tested so he knows she'll be all right or until he talks to her.

Pulling up to the club, I park my bike next to Mack's before heading inside.

No one is in the bar area, but I didn't expect them to be since it's still early. We may be bikers who like to drink and have a good time, but even we have standards.

Heading right to Mack's office, I don't bother to knock before entering. When the door opens, I see KitKat trying to right her shirt and skirt. Looks like someone was gettin' lucky this mornin'. I can't even remember the last time I've had good morning sex. Probably before that shit with The Street Kings. Now I probably won't get that back until after the baby's born. Or maybe I won't. Fuck, I hope it's not all true what they say about your sex life going downhill after having a kid.

Mack interrupts my worries by clearing his throat. "Out," he says, looking at me, but I know he's talking to Kit. I wonder what's going on with them. I've seen them together a few times, and I know for a fact that no one besides Mack fucks her, but he doesn't seem to be attached to her because he fucks other chicks when the opportunity presents itself. I'll have to ask him about it when shit quiets down more. I really want to see him happy and settle down. He's not old, but he's old enough that you'd think he'd want to find a woman and keep her.

When Kit closes the door behind her, I smirk at Mack. "Shut the fuck up and sit down. I want this shit dealt with and now," Mack growls. Obviously his morning fuck didn't help his mood any. He can be a grizzly bear in the morning. Maybe I should start calling him Grizzly. That thought makes me laugh, but thankfully Mack doesn't comment.

Sitting down in front of his desk I ask, "So what do you want to do with him? I don't think he took any of our threats to heart, so maybe we need to kick it up a notch to scare him outta town." I don't want to have to kill him, even though I'm sure Dani wouldn't care. I just worry that later on she would. Maybe when our child is grown or maybe she would decide to contact him and find out that I was a part of his demise.

Would she hate me?

Mack looks deep in thought, probably thinking the same thing that just went through my mind. "Set up another meet with him. We'll lay it out for him one last time. Tell him we'll make sure she's taken care of, but on our terms, not his. We'll give him twenty-four hours to vacate or else," Mack says, not looking happy about the *or else* part, but I know he'll do anything to make sure that Dani is protected, even from her birth father. We both would.

***

We're meeting Daniel at the clubhouse this time, hoping that by having our brothers surround us, he'll finally get the message to leave and never come back. The brothers may not know the specifics about what's going on, but they'll stand behind us no matter what and will follow our lead. They don't have to know who Daniel is or what he wants, though I'm betting they'll make the connection pretty quick. Dani does look a lot like her father.

Daniel walks into the bar at exactly one o'clock, looking around with what looks like confidence, but I can see the fear and uncertainty on his face. Good, maybe this won't be hard to do after all.

Mack walks up to him and tells him to follow him into his office. Daniel follows Mack and I follow Daniel. I glance around the club and see all our brothers looking on with hard looks, but I can tell they've figured it out already. They know who this man is.

I close the door a little harder than I needed to

when we all get into the office, but I get a smug satisfaction out of seeing Daniel jump from fear, but he tries to cover it up by coughing. Fucking idiot, he really has no idea how transparent he is. Glancing at Mack, I see a small smirk on his face so I know that he saw it as well.

When Daniel sits down in the only chair in front of Mack's desk, I stand right behind him, hopefully scaring him further. "All right, let's get down to business," Mack says with an edge in his voice.

"Have you told Danielle yet?" Daniel asks in what I assume he thinks is a hard voice, but he's not fooling anyone but himself.

"No, I haven't, and I don't plan to," Mack says. Daniel tries to speak, but Mack holds his hand up, silencing him. "You don't have a say in anything concerning Dani. She's *my* daughter and she's having Blaze's baby. You…you are nothing to her but a man who left her when she needed you most. So here's what you're going to do." Mack pauses for a short moment, looking at Daniel with threatening eyes. "When you walk out of my club, you're going to pack your shit and you're going to leave town. You won't ever try to contact Dani and you won't ever try to see her. You will leave California and never come back." I wait for him to continue because I know there's more. If not, I'll be sure to add my say. "If I find out you're even within one hundred miles of Dani, I'll find you and I'll bury you where no one will ever find your body. That's if I decide to leave enough of your body to find. You feel me?" Mack finishes.

When Daniel doesn't make a move to agree, I place my hand on his shoulder and squeeze tightly.

"Do. You. Fucking. Understand?" I growl, squeezing tighter with each word.

"*Yes!* Yes, I understand," Daniel says through the pain.

I squeeze once more to emphasize what we are telling him before releasing him. "Good. I'm glad we're on the same page. Now get the fuck outta my club and never show your face around here again," Mack says, then I haul Dani's piece of shit father out of the chair and push him out the door, knowing our brothers will make sure he finds his way to the door. We've already told Slayer to follow him to make sure he follows through and leaves. If he doesn't, he has orders to bring him back here so we can get rid of him ourselves.

CHAPTER 7

32 Weeks Pregnant

Dani

When I woke up this morning, I wasn't feeling well. I don't know if I'm just uncomfortable or if it's something else, but I just don't feel right. My head is hurting, my back aches, and I'm dizzy.

Walking downstairs, I head into the kitchen, hoping that something to eat will at least cure one of my ailments.

I was expecting to see Zane somewhere down here since he wasn't upstairs, but the house is empty. Looking outside, I see his bike is gone, so he must have left to either go to the club or he's gone to work.

He's decided he wants to start a security company, so he's been working on setting it up the past couple of weeks. I know Mack and Slayer have been helping him and I think a couple brothers from surrounding charters have come to help as well. I think it's a great idea and am so proud of him, though I wish he were home. I'm in my last trimester of pregnancy now and this will be all the alone time we'll have before we bring our child home.

Sitting at the table, I try to eat a bowl of cereal, but it's just not tasting good. Maybe I'll just stop at the café on my way in to the shop and pick up a green tea and bagel.

Going back upstairs, I dress in a pair of cut-off yoga shorts, a white tank-top that is probably too tight to be decent on a pregnant woman, and zip up one of Zane's black hoodies. Putting my hair into a ponytail, then pulling it through an old baseball cap, I'm ready to go. At least I'm wearing comfortable clothing. Maybe with this on, my body will finally relax and get the idea to follow suit. God, I can only fucking hope.

By the time I make it into the shop, Louie is already with his first appointment and Sara is on the phone, probably booking more business. That should make me happy, but I just can't get out of this black mood today. Maybe I should just go home, sleep the day away. I bet I'd feel better if I did that.

Sara interrupts my musings of playing hookie. "Morning, babe! Don't you look cute today," Sara says, too fucking chipper, if you ask me.

"Cute? I look fucking fat and uncomfortable, Sara, so don't try to sugarcoat this shit, it will only piss me off." I would feel bad for my tone, but I just can't find it in myself to care. I see her face fall at my words, which makes me want to cry. Fucking hormones! "I'm sorry, Sara, I didn't mean that," I say, blinking away tears.

She comes out from behind the desk and pulls me

in for a hug. "Yes, you did, and that's okay. I know how shitty you've been feeling lately. If you need a punching bag, hopefully only verbally though, I'm your girl." She ends with a smile full of pity. I hate when people pity me, but I already feel bad about being a bitch to her, I don't need to add to that. Then I'll not only hear about it from Toby, but I'll really start crying and will probably drown everything in the building.

"No, I'm fine, really. So what do I have today? Please tell me I'm not booked solid," I say, walking into my station with Sara following.

"Actually, you only have one appointment today. The one you had scheduled for this afternoon called to reschedule, but we just got a call for a walk-in. He should be here any minute, actually." Well, that's something. Maybe I really will go home after this appointment. I'm sure Louie can handle any other walk-ins that may come in.

"All right, just call for me when he gets here. Do you know what he wants?" I ask, going through my supplies to make sure I'm stocked since I didn't do it last night.

"The only thing he said was that it was a sleeve, but he's willing to do it in sessions," Sara answers before she walks back to the front of the shop.

Usually right about now I'd be jumping for joy and praying that I get to design whatever it is they want, but today, all I'm hoping for is that he has a stencil all ready for me and it's tribal or something easy.

Ten minutes later, I hear Sara call from the front that my appointment is here. Getting up from my stool takes a couple of tries, and once I'm standing, I have to grab onto the customer chair to steady myself. Yup, definitely going home after this.

I walk into the front and see a guy standing in front of the glass cases hanging on the wall that displays our flash tattoo designs. I can't see his face, but he's tall, tan, and muscular. He's wearing a hat that's backwards and a PT tank top.

When I clear my throat, he starts to turn toward me. "If you're ready, we can head—" I begin, but when I get a look at his face, I'm speechless. His eyes and the set of his mouth are so familiar to me, but I almost don't want to ask his name for fear that I'm wrong.

"Hello there, you must be the infamous Dani. I—" I cut him off.

"Jax?" I ask, both praying he'll confirm it and hoping I'm wrong. Jax became my best friend after Zane left for college. He was always there for me when I needed him. God, I haven't seen him since my grandmother's funeral. Is it really him?

"Uh, yeah, how did you know?" Jax asks, really focusing his eyes on my face now, trying to see if he knows me.

I don't give him time to try and figure it out though before I leap into his arms and cry. "Jax! I can't believe it's you," I sob, holding him tightly, afraid he'll disappear if I don't hold onto him.

I've thought of him a lot over the years, but never tried to find him. I just wanted my past to be just that; the past. I wanted to move on and be done with all that shit, but seeing him now, I realize how much I've missed him. Before I left for college, I heard he was down in Florida, so I have no idea why he's here.

Jax is stunned silent for a couple of seconds, either because he has no idea who the crazy pregnant woman is that's clinging to him for dear life or because he figured out who I am and can't believe it either.

Finally, he snaps out of it and pushes away from me, but not far, just enough so he can lean down and look into my eyes. "Danielle, is that you?" he says in disbelief. All I can do is nod my head, but that's enough for him. He wraps his arms around me again and holds me so tight I lose my breath, but I don't care. I can't fucking believe he's here in my shop!

The sound of someone clearing their throat breaks us out of our happy reunion. "Someone care to tell me what the fuck is going on out here?" Louie sounds pissed. Shit, I forgot he was here. I pull out of Jax's arms, but not far enough away that I can't put my arm around him. I don't want to let him go, I've missed him so much.

Looking from Jax to Louie, then back to Jax, I say, "Louie, this is Jaxon. We went to high school together and were best friends," I say in way of explanation, though it's not his fucking business, but I'm in a sharing mood. Anything that will get him off my back and let me catch up with Jax.

Louie, of course, having to argue with me about everything, says, "I thought Blaze was your best friend."

Cutting my eyes to him, I give him a hard look. "He was. Until he left to go to college, or the Marines, as it turned out. Jaxon and I started hanging out my junior year and stayed in touch when he left for college. Unlike some people," I add that last part quietly, not really meaning for everyone else to hear, but Jax catches it. When I look up at him, he gives me a confused look, but I just shake my head and whisper, "I'll tell you about it later."

Not needing to explain myself further, I pull Jax behind me toward my station. I want to be alone and know what he's been up to, how he's been, and why he's here in California. I hope he lives here and isn't just visiting. It would devastate me to just get him back in my life, only to lose him again.

***

Jax ended up not getting his tattoo today, settling for just sitting in the back room with me talking. He told me about Florida and that he left there about six months ago to move here. He's currently working a private security job that's only for a year, but he's hoping to find something so he can stay. He said even before he knew I was here he wanted to stay, he liked it here, but now having found me, he didn't think he'd be able to leave California. That news made me happy.

I told him about Zane, leaving out the bad parts, and just said that after my grandmother died, I tried college but couldn't stay there, so I came here. I told him about the MC and about all the amazing people I've met. How they're like my family.

Jax knows about my mother dying and my father leaving. He obviously knows about my grandmother dying and now knew that Zane went into the military, so I was pretty much alone. But I assured him that as soon as I moved here, I met Mack and everyone else,

43

and they became my family.

"Why didn't you just call me? You know I would have come home or, shit, at least offered you a place to crash at my place in Florida," Jax says when I'm done telling him everything.

"I just needed a fresh start, Jax. I'm sorry, I hope that doesn't upset you. It wasn't personal, and to be quiet blunt, I really wasn't thinking about anyone or anything, except getting the hell outta Dodge." I really hope he understands. It would kill me if he was mad or hurt that I didn't confide in him.

He smiles and grabs my hand. "I get it. Sometimes, you just have to start over and do things for yourself," he says, complete understanding in his eyes. I smile back and squeeze his hand. "I've missed you so much, Jax," I say, tears threatening to fall again, but I push them back.

"I've missed you too, Danielle," he replies, leaning forward and pulling me into another hug.

CHAPTER 8

33 Weeks Pregnant

Zane

This week has been hell, that's for sure.

When I went to pick Dani up at the shop last week, I walked in to see her cuddled up with some fucking guy. They were sitting on the couch; laughing, holding hands, and looking too fucking happy together.

When I hauled him up by his shirt and had my fist an inch from his face, Dani jumped up and yelled, "STOP!" It gave me enough pause that she was able to worm her way between us.

"Zane, stop. This isn't what it looks like. He's a friend—of both of us." That had me even more confused since I didn't know the fucker standing in front of me wearing that smug smile.

I let go of his shirt and pushed him back with a little too much force, which made his smile slip and mine grow. "The fuck he's a friend of mine," I said, looking at him and not Dani. I didn't want to take my eyes of the fucker in case he did something stupid.

"Zane, its Jax. You remember him—from high school? He played football with you," Dani says, starting to get attitude.

"Jaxon Reynolds?" I ask, the name vaguely ringing a bell. If I remember correctly, he was a year younger than me. He's also one of the guys I told to stay the fuck away from Dani. Okay, I lied. I actually told every guy in the school to stay away from her. Looks like someone didn't fucking listen.

Jaxon walks forward with his hand held out. "That's me, brother. Long time no see. How the hell have ya been?" he says. I stared at his hand with no intention of shaking it until Dani slapped my shoulder. When I looked down at her, she was glaring at me.

Sighing, I shook his hand. "Yeah, not fucking long enough," I said, which garnered another glare from Dani. Sorry, Baby Girl, you're just gonna have to deal with it.

Dani and Jaxon made plans to meet up the next day before we went home. The ride was silent and every time I looked over at her, she had a big smile on her face. Why the hell is she so fucking happy about this guy? I haven't seen her smile like that in months.

After we got home, we talked for a long time; how she and Jaxon became friends, how he was there for her when she needed someone, and how much she's missed him since coming here. She looked so sad when she told me she regretted leaving Texas and not telling him where she was going, but that she needed a new start. And now seeing how happy she is, how the fuck can I be mad about that? I can't, but I sure as fuck can tell him to keep his hands to himself from now on, otherwise he'll be missing a limb or two.

The last couple of days, Jaxon has been coming over a lot to help Dani with last minute baby shit. I was pissed at first, because that should be me doing that stuff with her, not him, but then I figured at least she's happy and safe. That has to count for something, right? I don't have to be one-hundred-percent happy about it, but it is what it is.

Tonight he's supposed to be coming over for dinner; I guess they both have something they want to talk to me about. What the fuck it is, I have no idea, but it has me on edge and pissed off. Not sure why I'm pissed, but ever since he's been around, that's been my mood more so than not, so fucking sue me.

Walking into the house, I can hear them laughing in the kitchen. Great, he's already here.

I don't even bother taking my shoes off, I just want to get in there and see my girl. What I see surprises the hell outta me. Dani is sitting at the kitchen table with her feet up on the chair next to her and Jaxon is cooking. I'm stunned. I know she's been tired lately and her feet have been hurting but I never thought he'd do something like this. I hate it, but it makes me have to like him even more, taking care of my girl like that.

"Hey, Baby Girl, how you feeling today?" I ask as I walk up behind her, then lay a kiss on the top of her head. When Jaxon looks at me over his shoulder, I nod my head in greeting. He gives me a look that says, "See, I'm not a bad guy." As much as I hate to admit it, he's really not. Over the last week, I've seen how close they are and it really is like a brother-sister relationship. Even though I still don't like it when he touches her in any way, I can see that he means nothing by it and she's never looked at him the way she looks at me. Maybe I should put this shit behind me. Seems like he's here to stay, so I don't really have much choice unless I want to cause problems with Dani and me, and that's something I will do anything to avoid.

"I'm tired, my feet are swollen and sore, and I'm fucking huge and uncomfortable. Other than that, I guess I'm okay," she says with a smirk. I know she's telling the truth, but she's trying not to be a bitch about it.

"Soon, babe, soon our son or daughter will be here and you'll forget all about how you feel right now." Fuck, I hope that's true. It's what I've read in books anyway.

She laughs and playfully shoves me away. "Whatever, fucker. You carry a baby around for nine months, have your body change in ways that shouldn't be possible, and then tell me that you can forget how you felt." I laugh with her, then grab her face and kiss her hard on the mouth.

"I may not be able to understand how you feel, but I can tell you that I love you and you look more beautiful every day." Maybe that's cheesy and a pussy thing to say, but she's my girl and it's the truth. She's fucking sexy carrying my child, and I'm not ashamed to say it or that I fucking love her.

"Kiss ass," she whispers with a smile on her face.

Standing up and walking over to the fridge, I take out two beers. I pop the tops on both, then hand one to

Jaxon. "Need any help, man?" I ask, feeling a little bad that he's in my house, cooking for me and my woman.

"Nah, I'm good. It's about done anyway," he says as he stirs what looks like some sort of stir fry. Damn, that smells good!

Setting my beer down, I grab plates and set them around the table. Not being able to resist, I drop another lingering kiss on Dani's lips, but we're interrupted by Jaxon clearing his throat. "All right, you two, that's enough. Wouldn't want me puking in the food, would ya?" Dani and I both laugh, and I'm suddenly reminded how things used to be with Dani, Zeke, and me. I wonder, if he never would have died, if we would still be here right now, but maybe minus Jaxon.

"Ha-ha, Jax." Dani laughs, making me shake my head to clear those thoughts. Zeke is gone and that's not gonna change. No use wondering what could have been.

Jaxon brings over the food and we all dig in. He and Dani talk about the tattoo he wants while I listen in. I love it when she talks about her work. She's so passionate; you can tell just by looking at her when she's talking about drawing or tattooing. I'm so grateful she was able to find Mack. Not just because she was safe and found a family in him and the club, but she was able to find what she truly loves to do. He did that for her. I'll never be able to repay him for what he's done for her, and ultimately, me.

When we're done eating, I stand to clear the table. Jaxon stands to help, but I wave him off. "I got it, man. You cooked so I'll clean up." I don't wait for him to answer, I just clear the table and put all the dishes in the dishwasher.

Sitting back down, it looks like Dani and Jaxon are having a silent conversation. Waiting a couple of moments, I wait to see if they're going to tell me what's going on, but when they don't, I ask, "What's going on?"

Dani gives Jaxon one last encouraging look before he looks at me. "Well, Dani was telling me about the company you're starting. Security, right?" he asks. Not sure where this is going and why he's interested, I just nod my head. "I'm not sure if you know this, but I came here for a temporary job. In security. I've been doing some work with private companies and some work with people who are in the media a lot." I still don't say anything, but I think I know where this is going. "Was wondering if you needed any help or were hiring," he says, leaving the last part hanging.

I make a show of thinking about it, but really, there's nothing to think about. I'm pretty much doing this by myself, but some of the brothers at the club have offered to do some jobs if needed. It'd be nice to have someone work with me that isn't a part of the club, that way if shit happens, I'll have someone on the outside that would always be available. "You got references?" I ask, not really caring either way. I've seen the way he is around Dani and can tell he'd be good at the job.

"Yeah, I can print out my resume and give it to you tomorrow if you'd like."

I shake my head. "Nah, don't worry about it. Why don't you come in next week and you can fill out some paperwork. I should have the office done by then," I say, looking over at Dani, who is smiling broadly at me.

"Yeah, sure thing. When do you think work will start?"

Thinking about everything that needs finished at the office, I answer, "Well, office won't be completely finished and ready to open till next month I'd guess, but we've already got some jobs lined up. If you're okay with it, I can contact them and we can start end of next week. Take on a few jobs before we actually open up." The more I think about it, the more I like the sound of that. With me doing all the work in the office myself, with a little help from the brothers, I haven't been able to do any jobs yet, telling them they'll have to wait till we open. But if Jaxon is game, then we can get started sooner than I thought.

"Yeah, I'm good with that," he says, then we spend the next fifteen minutes going over details while Dani just listens intently, offering a smile when we look over to her.

CHAPTER 9

34 Weeks Pregnant

Dani

Waking up, the first thing I notice is I'm alone in bed. Not like that is an odd occurrence lately, but I thought since things have been going well the past week maybe he'd be home more. Guess not.

Second thing I notice is my back is killing me. Well, more so than usual. Figuring I slept weird last night, I get out of bed and decide a long hot shower is in order.

Grabbing a pair of capri yoga pants and one of Zane's t-shirts, I head into the bathroom. I take my time washing my hair, then lather my loofah with my body wash and scrub my body. After that's all done, I wash my face then stand under the spray. I keep turning the knob every time the water starts getting colder, and don't get out till all the hot water is gone. Zane better hope he doesn't come home anytime soon for a shower 'cause he'll be shit outta luck.

Once out of the shower, I towel myself off and get dressed, then put some moisturizer on my face. Not wanting to take the time to dry my hair, I just braid it off to the side and I'm good to go. Slipping on a pair of flip-flops, since my feet are too swollen to wear anything else, I head downstairs to grab a water and orange for the road.

This will be my last week in the shop before I take the rest of my pregnancy off to get ready for the baby. Even though I pretty much have everything I need, I still want to go through everything, clean the house, and just prepare myself mentally. I never thought I'd be a mother, or at least have a baby without having my Gram around to help me. Maybe I should talk to Zane about having his mother come to visit. We used to be close; maybe she'd be able to help me get more comfortable with the idea and duties of being a mom. But Zane hasn't really talked much about his parents and I don't want to bring up bad memories if there's a reason he hasn't.

When I get in my truck, I realize I'm going to be early getting to the shop, but figure it will give me time to look at all the books and start getting things together and ready for when I'm gone. Mack said he'd stop by to make sure everything is going the way it should, and I know Louie and Sara will be fine on their own, but I still worry. In a way, that shop has been like my baby. Odd, I know, but it's the truth. I've put everything I am into that shop and I don't know what I'd do if I didn't have it anymore.

Just as I pull into my parking space in the back, I feel my phone vibrate next to me. Unlocking it, I see it's a text message from Jax.

Jax: Hey, Dani Girl. What you got planned for today?

Smiling at his use of the nickname some of the brothers use for me, I reply.

Me: Just getting some things done in the shop, getting ready to take my leave before the baby gets here. You?

Getting out of my truck, I make a mental note to talk to Zane about getting a new vehicle. I love my truck, but I think getting an SUV will be better with the baby. I'm still gonna keep my truck, but will only drive it when I'm by myself.

Unlocking the door to the shop, I step inside and then lock it again behind me so I don't get interrupted while doing some much-needed paperwork. I don't have any clients scheduled today and I think Louie has a pretty slow day as well. Actually, I don't think he's even scheduled to come in until later today. Either way, Sara and he both have a key, so when they get here, they'll be able to get in.

Sitting down at the front desk, I grab the schedule book and order book, then get up to head into my office. We've started getting everything transferred over to a computer system, but I still like having a paper copy of the schedules. Pisses Sara off to no end, but sometimes old school is the best way to do things. At least doing it like this, I know things won't get lost or deleted.

Once I'm in my office and sitting down, I hear my phone vibrate on the desk.

Jax: Heading to meet your boy now, then nothing. May stop by the shop to see ya. What ya think about getting lunch?

I start to type out my response, but I'm stopped suddenly by a sharp pain ripping through my stomach. What the hell was that? Breathing through the pain, I set my phone down to rub circles on my belly. Maybe the baby is just trying to get comfortable. It has to be getting pretty tight in there by now.

When the pain doesn't stop, only lessening a little, I try getting up and walking around my office. I've heard that sometimes if you walk around, it will lull the baby to sleep or at least settle them. But when I take my third step, another sharp pain brings me to my knees, tears instantly streaming down my face and a small cry slipping past my lips. Shit, this cannot be good. This can't be normal, can it? It's too fucking painful to be normal. Something is wrong. Something is really fucking wrong.

I try to stand to get to my phone and call Zane or the hospital, but when I make it to my feet, I can do nothing more than to fall back down when I feel a loud pop. Seconds later, I feel a gush of fluid soak through my pants and pool around me on the floor. Hearing my phone vibrate, I try to take deep breaths so I don't freak out any more than I am already. I need to calm down so I can get to my phone, but when I look down and see nothing but blood, I can do nothing but scream. There's so much blood. It's so thick and dark that it looks black. And the smell! It smells like wet rust and leaves a weird taste in my mouth.

Knowing I need to get someone here to help me, I try with everything I have to get up to grab my phone, but I'm dizzy and hurting. I don't even make it halfway to my feet before I'm falling. Before I can even try to catch myself to cushion my fall, my eyes close involuntarily and I can do nothing but just let it happen. There's nothing but numbness overtaking my body and darkness. At least here in the nothingness, there's no pain.

***

Jax

After a couple minutes with no reply from Dani, I decide to text her again. She could just be busy, but knowing how far along she is, I don't like it when she doesn't answer me.

Me: Dani Girl, you there?

There, simple and to the point. Zane and I have talked quite a bit since last week. He told me about the time Dani didn't answer her phone and he thought the worst. Turns out, she was just with a customer, but he said after that day, she knows to always answer her phone or text messages so we all know she's okay. May piss her off to no end and we may be in for it when we *do* hear from her, but I'll take that any day instead of not knowing if she's all right.

A few minutes later, there's still no response, so I call her. I'm already in my car and heading to the shop, but I'm getting a bad feeling. Speeding up to get to the shop faster, I dial her number.

Her phone rings four times, then it goes right to voice mail. I don't leave a message, but instead re-dial and pray that she's just on the phone or with someone. *Just answer the phone, Danielle. Let me know you're okay.* I say this over and over while I listen to her phone ring and ring before going to voice mail again. Fuck! Something is wrong, I just know it.

Stepping on the gas, I swerve around cars and people walking the streets, now only a few blocks away from the shop. As soon as I get there, I park in the front and don't even bother to turn my car off.

Running up to the door, I try the handle but it's locked. "Fuck!" I yell and start to bang on the door. "Dani! Dani, open up!" I quit banging for a second and try to see if I can hear her inside, but I get nothing.

Not knowing what else to do, I kick the door in. "Dani! Where are you, honey?" I yell out, running through every room in the shop, but still not finding her.

Coming up to the last door in the back, I take a deep breath before opening the door. The sight in front of me has my heart stopping. Dani's lying on the floor, unconscious, and there is so much blood surrounding her body. And it's coming from between her legs. Dear God, please let her and the baby be okay. That's the only thought I have as I lift her up and run with her out to my car. "It's gonna be all right, Danielle. I've got you...I've got you," I whisper as tears roll down my face. Once I have her in the car, I hightail it toward the hospital.

CHAPTER 10

Fifteen Minutes Later

Zane

I'm trying to get the rest of this room done so I can get home and cook for Dani. She's been so uncomfortable these last few weeks and seeing what Jax did last week for her and how happy it made her to not have to do anything makes me want to do it for her as well. Though, I'm going to do one better and pamper her all night. First with dinner, then I'll run her a bath, then I'm going to rub her back and feet for her. That will make her happy and hopefully feel a little better as well.

As I sand the rest of the putty off the wall so I can start painting, I hear my phone ring. "Yeah?" I ask into the phone, hoping whatever it is isn't something that needs my immediate attention. I've left the surveillance of The Street Kings to my brothers, but if something goes down, they'll need me to help take care of the problem. I'm just hoping that's not what this phone call is about. I don't want to have to stop what I'm doing or risk not being able to fulfill my plan for tonight. But my hopes are dashed as soon as I hear Louie's frantic voice on the other end.

"It's Dani! She's gone and there's blood everywhere!" The words Dani, gone, and blood are the only words that filter through my head.

"What the fuck do you mean she's gone and there's blood everywhere? What the hell happened and where the fuck is my woman?" I yell back into the phone, already running out to my bike. If something happens to her or our baby, I don't think I'll be able to go on. She and that baby are everything to me.

"I don't fucking know! I came in and the door was busted in. When I searched the place, I found blood in her office and her purse and phone on her desk. I don't know what happened! Just get here. Now!" he growls, though I know it's not directed at me, but the situation. Dani is his best friend, but she's the love of my life, so if anyone should be freaking out, it should be me. "Besides the door, does it look like there was a struggle?" I ask, needing all the information I can get.

I keep the phone plastered to my ear even though I'm now driving eighty to get to the shop. It doesn't seem to faze Louie, though. "No, brother, doesn't look like there was a struggle, but who the fuck knows? They could have taken her by surprise or maybe it was someone she knew," he says in a hurry. Then I hear him say away from the phone, probably to another brother, "Get Mack on the phone and start putting calls out. Find her!" I don't say anything else to him, I just keep driving, but keep the connection with him, not wanting to slow down or put any focus into putting my phone away.

A few minutes later, I'm pulling up to the shop and see Mack, Louie, Toby, Sara, Skinner, and Tom Tom standing out front, yelling at each other. Well, everyone but Sara. She's just standing there with her arms wrapped around her middle, crying.

When I make it to them, Louie and Mack look at me with both anger and pain in their eyes. "Anything?" I ask, walking into the shop and back toward her office.

"We've got nothing, brother. But everyone is out looking and I've called in some favors to help find her," Mack says.

"Where's Slayer? Does he still have eyes on her piece of shit father?" I ask as we hurry toward Dani's office. I don't think her father would do something to harm her, but if he were desperate enough, maybe he would. Who knows at this point. I don't know her father from Adam, so he could be some psycho and I wouldn't even know.

"I called him as soon as I found out. Daniel hasn't left Michigan since he got back," he says just as we reach her office.

The scene before me looks like something out of a horror film: there's blood covering a huge portion of the floor and then there are shoe prints leading out of the room. When I turn to look back out into the hallway, I see bloody hand prints.

Suddenly, I feel so beaten down and drained. I should have been here. She's God only knows where, hurt, and I have no idea how to even begin looking for her.

My phone rings, interrupting my pity party, and I answer. "Did you find her?" I ask, not looking to see who is calling.

Jaxon starts talking through the phone, but I can't understand him. Is he crying? "Dani...blood...found her..." That's pretty much all I've been able to make out, but it sends relief through my body, giving me enough hope and will power to snap the fuck out of it and get to my girl.

"Where is she? Is she all right? Is the baby all right? How did you find her? What happened?" I ask the questions in rapid succession.

"We're at the hospital. You need to get here fast. I think there's something wrong with the baby and no one will fucking tell me anything!" he says, now sounding angry.

I hang up the phone without even saying goodbye, then turn toward Mack. "She's at the hospital. Jaxon thinks it's the baby," I say before running outside and racing like a bat outta hell to get to the hospital.

Everyone follows me and but I don't slow down to wait for them. Dani and the baby need me.

***

The drive to the hospital seems to take hours, but in reality, I make it there in less than ten minutes. I'm not stopping for anything, even if a pig flashes his cherries at me. They'll just have to wait. My brothers stay right on my tail the whole time, but I barely even notice them, too lost in thought and praying that my family is okay.

When I pull up to the doors, I almost flatten my

bike on the asphalt with how fast I stopped and jumped off, barely putting my kickstand up, but I couldn't care less.

I run up to the nurses' station on the first floor with my brothers right behind me. "My girl was just brought in. She's pregnant and bleeding." My voice is raised and people are looking at me.

The nurse looks at me with annoyance. "Name, please."

"Danielle DeChenne. Are her and the baby all right?" I ask, getting pissed that she doesn't just point me to where I can find my girl.

"Are you family?" the nurse says, looking at me sternly.

"She's pregnant with my fucking baby. Just tell me where the fuck she is!" I yell, leaning over the desk. I want to reach out and wrap my hands around this bitch's throat, force her to show me where Dani is.

"Sir, if you don't calm down, I'll have to ask you to leave." You'd think she'd be scared with a pissed off biker yelling at her, especially when he's backed by at least three more, but no. She's still speaking with annoyance, like I'm a fucking ant that she thinks she can crush under her shoe.

"If you don't tell me where the fuck—" I start to yell, but Mack comes up and places his hand on my shoulder, holding me back.

"You need to calm down. Dani and the baby need you right now. You won't be able to do anything for them if your ass is locked away in a jail cell." I hate that he's right, but the bitch nurse better start talking real fucking soon before I get so pissed off I start ripping this place apart and none of my brothers will be able to hold me back.

When Mack see's that I'm calmer, he turns toward the nurse. "Ma'am, I'm sorry, but we're the only family she has. Please just tell us where she is and if she and the baby are all right." The nurse looks a little less irritated when she looks at Mack, but as soon as her eyes find mine again, they go hard.

Looking back to Mack, she says, "She's on the fourth floor, but you'll have to wait in the waiting area. She's in surgery right now. That's all I know. The doctor will come and find you when they have more news."

Without waiting for anything else, I push my way to the stairs, ignoring Mack calling out for me to stop, and run up the stairs two at a time.

Barging into the waiting room, I see Jaxon hunched over a chair in the back. There's no one else in the room, which I'm glad about. They'd probably just leave when they see all the bikers anyway.

"What happened? Did someone hurt her?" I ask Jaxon, needing to know everything.

He looks up and I can see that he's trying to hold back his tears. "I don't know, man. We were texting and I asked if she wanted to grab lunch. When she didn't reply, I called, but got no answer. I just knew something was wrong, so I went to the shop as fast as I could. The door was locked and she wasn't answering, so I kicked it in. When I got to her office, she was just lying there, unconscious. There was so much blood—"

"Did it look like someone attacked her?" I interrupt, not really wanting to hear about all the blood she lost. I fucking saw her office, I know what it looked like.

Jaxon shakes his head. "No. I think it was something to do with the baby."

After he says that, I can do nothing but just drop to the floor. I've read all the books. I wanted to prepare myself for anything I would need to know for Dani's pregnancy and awaiting our baby, so I know all the things that can go wrong.

I feel someone come up to me and place their hand on my shoulder. "They'll be okay. Dani is strong, she's a fighter. So is the baby. You need to stay strong, Blaze. They're going to need you soon." I can barely make out that it's Louie talking to me, he speaks so low and I can tell that he's holding back emotion of his own.

"It's too early...it's too early," I whisper, knowing that if she delivers now, there's a possibility the baby won't make it.

I know my girl is a fighter. She's been through so much worse so I know she's going to be okay. I just hope our baby takes after her and will fight too.

CHAPTER 11

Two Hours Later

Zane

Zeke, if you can hear me, I need you now, brother. I'm sorry I was so angry at you when you left and hated you when you died. I just couldn't see why you felt the need to do what you did, but even though I never told you, I'm so very proud of you and I miss you every day.

But today isn't about me. Dani and our unborn baby is in trouble. I don't know what happened, or if they are even okay, but I need you to be with them. I need you to give them strength and courage to fight whatever it is they need to fight to come back to me. I need them, Zeke. I need them like I needed you, but I know if I lose them too, I won't be able to live anymore.

Please help them, Zeke. I can't be there right now for them, but you can. Please, brother. Please save them.

***

For the past two hours, I've done nothing but kneel on this floor and pray to God that my girl and baby are okay. I've pleaded with my brother to help them. I've begged God to let me take their place. I've willed the doctor to come in and tell me my family is all right.

I haven't looked up into the eyes of my brothers, afraid of what I'll see. I don't want to see their fear that Dani and the baby are gone. I don't want to see their hope that they're okay and still with me. And I don't want to see their pity. I can't deal with any of it, so I just stare at the ground in front of me.

When I hear the door to the waiting room open, I glance up and see a man in scrubs walk in. Jumping to my feet, I hurry toward him.

"Please tell me Dani and my baby are okay," I plead in a broken voice. I have no idea if he's here about Dani, but seeing as to how no one else is here waiting for news, it has to be.

"Are you her husband?" the doctor asks.

"Yes," I say, hoping he doesn't question me.

The doctor looks behind me to where I assume all my brothers are standing, waiting like me for news.

"Dani suffered from a placental abruption. This is when the placenta separates from the uterus before the baby is born. It can be minor, but in Dani's case, the placenta was completely separated from her uterus, which caused severe blood loss. We had to perform an emergency C-section since this could cause serious complications."

The doctor doesn't say anything else and I find

myself getting pissed the longer he doesn't tell me that Dani and the baby are okay.

"Is the baby okay?" I say as calmly as I can, but Mack can hear the edge in my voice, so he places his hand on my shoulder, silently telling me to calm down.

"Well, one of the babies is just fine; breathing on his own and only seems to be a little underweight," the doctor says.

Shocked, I have no idea what to say. Did he just say *babies*? As in, there's more than one? Thankfully, Mack takes over asking the questions.

"You mean to tell us Dani gave birth to more than one baby?" I hear the surprise in his voice, but I also hear excitement. When he found out Dani was pregnant, he was over the moon happy. Now, knowing there's more than one baby, he's got to be fucking thrilled. But I can't be happy about it. Not yet. I need to know that they all are okay.

"Yes. Twins, actually," the doctor says this evenly, like it's every day he drops a bomb like this on people, like it's normal for them to think they're only having one baby, then wind up having two.

"How is that possible? We only heard one heartbeat, saw only one baby on the ultrasound," I say, trying to wrap my mind around the fact that I'm now a father of *two*.

"It doesn't happen often, but sometimes, the second baby can hide behind the other. That's the case here, but it's also because your daughter is a lot smaller than her brother. That may be why they didn't know Dani was carrying twins," the doctor explains, but I think I only heard the word *daughter*. I have a son and a daughter.

"You said she was smaller than her brother. But she's fine, right?" I think that's Louie, but I can't be sure. I'm still reeling from the news of twins, of having a son and daughter.

"She's smaller by two pounds. Now, that may not sound like much, but for a baby, it's the difference between a hundred pounds and two hundred pounds. But it's not the weight that's concerning us right now. She's not able to breathe on her own, so we have her hooked up to a machine that does that for her. She also isn't able to eat the way normal babies can, so we have a tube that will feed her so she'll gain the weight she needs to get stronger. She'll have to stay in the NICU for a couple of weeks, but if she puts on the weight and the steroids we gave her to help develop her lungs work as they should, she'll be fine to go home and shouldn't have any long term complications. As far as your son, he'll stay in the NICU with his sister tonight, and given that he continues eating and keeping his body temperature up, he'll be able to stay with you until he's released in a few days."

A huge weight is lifted now that I know the babies are going to be fine. I still can't believe we have two. I can't wait to tell Dani.

Smiling, I ask, "Have you told Dani we have a son and a daughter? When can I go see her?" She's going to freak when she finds out if they haven't told her already. But I know she's going to be so happy.

The doctor's face falls marginally, but it's enough that I can tell that what he's about to say isn't good.

"You can see her soon, but she's in a coma. She

lost a lot of blood before she got here and even more during the delivery. We've given her two blood transfusions, but during that time, she started having seizures due to her extremely high blood pressure. We were able to stop them, but we couldn't do anything until we got the babies out. I'm not sure yet what the damage is, but it could've caused minor brain damage. I've scheduled her for an MRI tomorrow to look for any swelling or abrasions, but for now, the only thing we can do is wait until she wakes up."

And my whole world just dropped. I feel like I've just taken a ride on the most deadly of roller coasters. Sure, they're not meant to be deadly, but they take you up so high and make you feel like you are on top of the world. Then they bring you down faster than your organs can keep up with or so fast that the car will slide off the tracks or you fall out, falling to your death. That's the way I feel right now. I was so high, then when I thought there was no way I'd come down, the car loses traction and falls at a rapid pace toward the ground, and you're dead.

But I'm very much still alive, it just *feels* like I'm dead. My whole world feels like it's being ripped away from me.

Zeke, please...please don't let Dani die. Please don't take her away from me. I will do anything, just please let her be okay. We have a son and a daughter now. They need her. I need her. Please, Zeke, help her come back to us.

CHAPTER 12

Two Days Old

Zane

The past two days have been Heaven and Hell. Our son was able to go into the regular nursery last night and has been doing great. Our daughter still can't breathe or eat on her own, but the doctors and nurses say she's doing very well. They think that by the end of the week she'll be able to come off the machines. But Dani still hasn't woken up yet.

They took her in for an MRI yesterday and it showed minimal swelling and there's some fluid built-up, but no abrasions. They say if the swelling doesn't go down, they'll have to go in and put in a shunt to drain the fluid in hopes that that will help with the swelling.

I've prayed more times than I think I have in my whole life. I've even taken to asking God to make Dani better. Since Zeke died, I've found it really hard to believe there was a God and have taken to just talking to Zeke. But willing to do whatever it takes for Dani to come back to me and get well again, I've been going to the chapel inside the hospital and praying. I've apologized for the years of not believing in Him and being angry that He took my brother away too soon. I've confessed all my sins and promised to never turn my back on Him so long as He brings my Baby Girl back to me and our children. I know that you should never give Him an ultimatum, but I don't know what else to do. I'm grasping at straws here, willing to do just about anything to have her open her eyes and be okay.

The nurse interrupts my thoughts. "How's she doing today?" I find it funny that a nurse is asking me how Dani is doing, but I recognize her as one of the nurses in the nursery, so she probably doesn't know about Dani's condition.

"No change," I say quietly. Even though I know she's in a coma and not just sleeping, I still try to keep my voice down. I don't want to disturb her, thinking maybe if she gets some much needed rest, she'll come back to me faster.

"She'll wake up soon. In the meantime, your son is awake. Thought I might stop by and see if you wanted to sit with him." The mention of my son puts a smile on my face, even though I still wish Dani was awake to see him too.

"Yeah, I was planning on heading up there shortly. I want to stop by and see how my little girl is doing first though." With any luck, they'll be able to take all the machines and wires off of her soon so I can actually hold her. They've said that I can now, but I'm too worried that I'll mess something up, so I've settled for just reaching my hand in and rubbing her back or holding her little hand. It makes me happy and sad at the same time every time I take her hand—her fingers barely reach all the way around my pinky finger.

The nurse smiles at me. "She's doing so well I hear. She's a fighter, just like her mama." At that, I can only nod, afraid if I say anything my emotions will get the best of me.

After the nurse leaves, I stand up and run my finger down the side of Dani's face. "You need to wake up, Baby Girl. Our son and daughter can't wait to meet their mama." I lean down and kiss her softly on the lips, wishing with all my might that I feel even the slightest twitch of her lips, but there's nothing. Pulling away, I kiss her forehead. "I love you. I'll be back soon."

On my way out the door, I'm surprised to see Mack. My brothers and Jaxon have all stopped by a few times to check in on Dani and sit with her sometimes while I go see the babies, and Mack has gone with me a few times to visit my son, but they won't allow him in the NICU.

"Hey. I was just getting ready to head upstairs," I say, not sure if he's here just for a visit or club business.

"Tell them Papa loves them. I'll sit with our girl 'til you get back." He's already taken to calling himself Papa, but it suits him.

I clasp him on the back on my way by, grateful that he's here. I hate leaving Dani alone, afraid she'll wake up and no one will be there, but sometimes there's nothing I can do.

I take the elevator up to the sixth floor where the NICU is. After the nurses buzz me in, I walk right over to where I know my daughter will be. "Hello, beautiful, how's Daddy's girl today?" I whisper to her before leaning down and placing a gentle kiss on her cheek. She's asleep, so I don't want to touch her too much and wake her up. She needs all the rest she can get so she can build up her strength.

One of the nurses comes over and checks her vitals. "She's doing very well. If she keeps this up, I would say in a few days she'll be in the nursery with her brother." I nod and smile, having no words to express how happy that makes me. If only her mother would wake up now, then life would be perfect.

"Have you given her a name yet?" the nurse asks once she writes whatever information she just got onto the clipboard.

"No. I'm waiting for her mama to wake up so we can decide together." It seems I get asked this question by every person who works here, like it's unusual for a baby not to be named right away or like I'm insane for waiting for Dani to wake up. But how could they even think I'd name the babies without her? When she was pregnant, we never discussed names. We knew that as soon as we saw our baby, now babies, we'd know what to name them. So I don't even have the smallest clue what Dani would like or not.

"I understand completely."

Not really caring what she understands or not, I don't reply back.

After spending a few more minutes with my daughter, I decide to head down to sit with my son.

Maybe I'll get to feed him again today. Yesterday the nurse was just getting ready to feed him when I walked in. Let's just say it was a challenge, but something that made me feel so much closer to him. I can now see why mothers love breastfeeding and how they say it helps them bond. But I'd give up my bonding time during feeding in a heartbeat for Dani to wake up and take the reins on that job.

When I get to the nursery where my son is, the nurse is just finishing up changing his diaper. Good, that's one thing I'm not ready for.

"Oh, hello there. Here to see our little guy, I take it." I've never seen this nurse before, but I'm sure the others have told her about the biker dad.

"Sure am," I say as I reach out for him just as she holds him out for me to take.

Once he's in my arms, I feel a peace settle over me. Even though his sister is still fighting to be able to breathe and eat on her own and his mother is still sleeping, holding him lets me know that things will be all right. His sister will get stronger and his mother will wake up.

"Hey, buddy. Did you miss your daddy?" I say, cradling him against my chest. He makes a small noise that is almost like a coo and I laugh. "I missed you too," I answer back.

I sit and rock him for a while, but he starts getting restless, so I flag one of the nurses down. "Does he need to eat?" I'm not good at telling what he needs and since I only know that he was just changed, he could be fussing because he's hungry, tired, or just cranky, for all I know.

"No, he was fed right before we changed him."

Not knowing what else to do, I get up and start walking with him, hoping that will settle him down, which seems to work some.

"Can I take him down to his mother's room? I'd like to get back, but don't want to leave him just yet," I say after five minutes of walking around the nursery. I do want to get back to Dani, but also, I want him to meet his mother, even though she's sleeping and he may not know who she is.

"Of course. If you put him in the crib, I'll roll him down to you in a few minutes. He can even stay the night down there with you if you'd like," the nurse replies with a smile.

I'm not sure if I'm ready to take care of him all on my own yet over night, but I just smile and lay him down in his crib. "Daddy will see you soon, bud. Then you get to meet your mama."

CHAPTER 13

Four Days Old

Dani

I'm dreaming I'm holding my baby, but he's crying and I have no idea what to do for him. I feel so helpless. What mother doesn't know how to make her baby stop crying?

Then out of nowhere I hear Zane hum. I don't know how I know it's him because I don't think I've ever heard him hum a day in his life, but I just know it's him. And it seems to be working. The baby settles down and stops crying. It makes me want to smile because I just knew Zane would be an amazing father, but sad because I couldn't get him to stop crying and it makes me feel like a failure.

"Shhh...it's okay, little guy, Daddy's got you," I hear Zane whisper and I'm at my breaking point. Hearing him talk so quietly and sweetly to our son, hearing the love in his voice, makes me break down in tears. But when I try to cry, nothing happens. I can feel them there, but they won't fall. What is wrong with me?

I try to move, but it's like my body is being held down and I don't know why. Why can't I move? I realize then that I can't see Zane or our baby, so I try to open my eyes, but just like my body, they won't move. I can feel my heart racing and a panic attack coming. Something is wrong with me! Why won't my body do what I want it to do?

And then it all comes back to me: being at the shop…the pain…and all the blood. *No!* The baby!

Suddenly, I feel hands on my face. "Dani? What's wrong, Baby Girl? Open your eyes," Zane says urgently. I try to listen and comply, but my eyes won't open and it makes me freak out even more. By now, my heart feels like it's one steady beat it's beating so fast.

I hear an alarm go off and feet running, but I still can't open my eyes. Please! Someone help me—why can't I open my eyes?

"What's happening?" Zane yells at someone and then I hear a baby cry. Is that my baby? Is he all right? I didn't think my heart could possibly beat any faster, but not knowing if that's my baby and if he's okay causes it to beat so hard and fast it feels like it's going to beat right out of my chest.

I feel something cool go into my arm and then my head feels fuzzy. *No!* "I need to know if my baby is okay," I want to scream, but I can't. I can't fight off the heaviness that's sinking me further and further away from my son and Zane and into the darkness.

***

I hear hushed voices. I can't make out who's talking or what they are saying, but I hear their tone. Whoever is talking is worried.

I try wiggling my toes and when I feel them finally cooperate, I try moving my hand. That seems to be working too.

Slowly opening my eyes, I'm blinded by a bright light. I don't know if it's the sun shining into my room or if the lights in here are just really fucking bright, but I have to close my eyes again because it hurts too much. I groan in pain.

The voices quiet and a couple of seconds later I feel someone grab my hand. I can tell before he even talks that it's Zane with the only way his touch makes me feel. "Dani?" he whispers close to my ear.

I turn my head slowly toward him but don't open my eyes again. "Too bright," I croak, my mouth dry and my throat screaming after I speak the words.

"Fuck, you're awake! Thank God. You had me so scared, Baby Girl." At the word baby, I remember what happened the last time I was awake.

"The baby! Zane, where's our baby?" I say, my eyes flying open, searching his face even though the brightness still burns my retinas.

"Hey, calm down. Everything is fine, just calm down." At his words, I'm able to settle down a little bit, but now I'm anxious to see my baby. Where is he? Why isn't he in the room?

My eyes start to hurt again, so I close my eyes and try to calm myself down more. The beeping from the heart monitor is going crazy. The sooner I calm down, the sooner he'll tell me about the baby and then hopefully I can go see him.

Zane catches on that the sun is hurting my eyes and looks at someone on the other side of my bed. "Close the blinds," he says then looks back at me. "How do you feel?"

I try to think about that and do a quick inventory of all my body parts. I can move my arms and legs and nothing hurts there. My head hurts a little bit, but it's my throat and stomach that hurt the most.

"Water," I say hoarsely, needing something to soothe my throat before I try talking more.

Zane places a mug of water in front of my lips. I sip tentatively at first, but once the water goes down my throat, I realize how thirsty I am, so I drink a little faster.

"Slow down, Baby Girl. Don't want to take too much and make yourself sick." I want to slap him, but he's probably right.

"I'll go grab the doctor and call everyone to let them know she's awake," I hear Louie say. I try to turn my head to look at him and smile, reassure him that I'm okay, but I can't seem to move fast enough before he's already out the door.

I frown, wondering why he didn't even say hi or seem even the slightest bit happy that I'm awake.

Zane, of course being able to tell what I'm thinking, answers before I can say anything. "He'll be all right. It just really shook him up what happened." Understanding dawns on me and I can see now why he didn't even look at me. Louie is my best friend, aside from Zane. Of course he would be really upset that something could have happened to me and the baby.

"He's the one who found me, isn't he?" I ask,

thinking that may be another reason he's so upset, but Zane shakes his head.

"Actually, it was Jaxon. He rushed you to the hospital, but no one knew what happened to you. Then Louie showed up at the shop and saw the blood. You really gave us all a scare, Baby Girl." I feel awful about what happened and what I must have put everyone through, but again, hearing him say baby nudges those maternal feelings in me—I need to see our child.

I nod and take one more drink of the water. "Please take me to our baby." I don't know how much longer I'll be able to stand not meeting my son.

Zane gets this look on his face, something between excitement and caution, and just as I think he's going to tell me, a doctor walks in with Mack right behind him.

"Well, hello there. Finally decided to wake up and join us, huh?" the doctor says with a warm smile. His words have me realizing I have no idea how long I was asleep.

"How long was I out?" I don't remember anything besides being in pain at the shop and passing out. Then I remember waking up and hearing my baby before I was out of it again. How long ago was that? The only thing I know is that I'm in a hospital, I'm no longer pregnant, and that I need to see my baby.

"You came in four days ago. You had a placental abruption, which caused you to lose a lot of blood. We did an emergency C-section, but during delivery, you starting having seizures, which caused your brain to swell and fluid to build up. You've been in a coma for the past four days, but the swelling and fluid have gone down almost all the way and everything looks good. Congratulations, by the way. You have a very healthy baby boy and a smaller, but getting healthier by the hour, baby girl."

I just stare at him, waiting for him to say he's joking or for Zane to tell him that he must have the wrong patient. I didn't have twins; I was pregnant with only *one* child. He has to have that wrong. But Zane just looks at me with the same expression on his face and when I look to Mack, he's smiling bigger than I think I've ever seen him smile.

"Um, can you repeat that? I don't think I heard you right. I thought you said we have a son *and* a daughter, but that can't be right," I say with a strained laugh.

The doctor laughs, but Zane's the one who answers. "Baby Girl, I know it's a shock. Shit, I was confused too, but it's true. We have a son and a daughter, and they are both perfect." I can see on his face that he's telling the truth and I can tell how excited and happy his is.

I feel tears rolling down my cheeks, but I think they are happy tears. I smile. "I want to see them." Zane just nods and then looks to the doctor.

"Absolutely. I just want to do a quick check on you and then I'll have a nurse bring in a wheelchair to take you up to see your babies." Not able to say any more, I just nod.

Ten minutes later, I'm sitting in a wheelchair, nervous and excited to meet my son and daughter for the first time since they were born four days ago.

CHAPTER 14

Four Days Old

First Meeting

Dani

Zane takes me to the NICU first to see our daughter. I'm told that she was smaller and less developed than her brother, but she's doing remarkably well. She's already gained almost a pound since she's been born and they think she'll be able to able to go off the breathing machine as soon as tomorrow. Once she's breathing on her own, they'll see if she can eat by herself, and if she does well with that, it will only be a matter of days before we'll be able to take her home.

When I first see my daughter, I start to cry. It's hard to see your son or daughter looking so small and have all sorts of tubes and wires connected to her.

"Shh…don't cry, Baby Girl. She'll be fine. She's a fighter, just like her mama," Zane says close to my ear as he kneels down and takes me into his arms. His words just make me cry even harder. She shouldn't have to fight. She should have been able to stay inside my womb until she was ready for the world, but I couldn't keep her there. I feel like I failed her somehow.

I calm myself down, knowing it's not helping anything. I look up at one of the nurses who also looks to have tears in her eyes. "Can I hold her?" I ask, not sure if that's even possible with all the wires hooked to her.

"Of course you can," she says with a smile, then gently picks her up, maneuvering around all the wires.

When she's placed in my arms, I feel a piece of my heart go out to her. This is my daughter, a part of me and Zane. It's hard to believe how much love I already have for her. She looks like a mixture of both of us too. She has my nose, but her father's mouth. I pray that she'll have his eyes too.

"Hello there, my little angel. I'm your mama," I say quietly. At my voice, she opens her eyes and stares right at me, like she already knows who I am. I feel another tear trail down my cheek and then Zane reaches out and wipes it away.

I look to him and watch as he strokes our daughter's back while she's perched on my chest. "How's Daddy's little girl today? See who I brought with me? Your mommy is awake and couldn't wait to meet you," he says in the gentlest voice I've ever heard him use.

We sit like this for what seems like hours—me holding our daughter with him looking between us while he never moves his hand off her back.

"Did you name her?" I ask, just now realizing I have no idea if she has a name or if we need to come up with one. We never talked about names before, so I don't know what Zane thinks we should name her. I honestly never thought we'd have a girl, so I never even thought of girl names.

"Of course I haven't named her yet. We were waiting for you," he says, smiling at me.

"What should we name her then? I haven't even thought of any girl names to be honest," I tell him, feeling like we need to name her right now before another minute passes.

Zane is thoughtful for a minute before he speaks. "Well, I thought of a couple names." I smile at him, encouraging him to tell me the names he likes.

"I was thinking either Rose after your mom and Gram, or Harley since we found each other again through the MC." I feel tears threaten to fall again at the mention of both names. I can't believe he put so much thought into this, but I guess he's had more time to think about it than I have. Or heck, maybe he's been thinking about them for a while.

Thinking the names over for a bit, I throw in my thoughts. "What about Harley Rose? That way, we can use both names." After saying the name out loud, I fall even more in love with it and think it's perfect for our daughter. And by the look on Zane's face, I can tell he likes it too.

"I think it's perfect, Baby Girl. Just like her and her mama." He leans over and kisses me softly on the lips, then leans down and kisses Harley on the top of her head. "Does that sounds good to you, Harley Rose?" he asks to our daughter. She must like it because she looks up into her father's eyes and I swear I see a smile grace her beautiful face.

We spend another hour just sitting there with her. Zane tells me he hasn't held her yet, that he was too scared to pull on the wires and tubes.

I ask the nurses to bring a chair over and once he sits down beside me, I situate her into her father's arms. He looks worried at first, but after a minute of nothing going wrong, he seems to relax a bit and just enjoys holding his daughter for the first time. I'm actually kind of glad that he hadn't held her yet. I wasn't only able to be the first to hold her, but I'm able to see the look on his face when he held her for the first time.

I know he's already held our son, so I won't be able to see the first time he held him and bonded with him, but at least I get *this* first. I missed so much being asleep for the past four days, but now I'll have the rest of my life to live out all the firsts for the little family we've created.

CHAPTER 15

Four Days Old

Watching Mommy Meet Her Son

Zane

For some reason, I feel a little more anxious taking Dani to meet our son than I did when we went to the NICU to see Harley. Maybe it's because I feel closer to our son than I do to our daughter, though that can't be right because I should feel the same way about both of them. I *do* feel the same way about both of them. But I've been able to spend more time with our son and I've been able to actually bond with him. Yeah, maybe that's it.

Walking into the nursery, I see the nurse that usually takes care of our son laying him down, but she stops and a huge smile overtakes her face when she notices me walk in. But when she sees I'm not alone today and I have Dani with me, the smile drops instantly and a small frown takes over her face, but it's gone just as fast.

"Hello there. Who do we have here?" she asks. There's something in her voice but I can't place it. Maybe it's just that I've never been here with anyone else or maybe she's just surprised that Dani is up and about after just waking up from being in a coma for the last four days. I couldn't care less, though. I have my girl, we just spent time with our daughter, and now I'm here to introduce our son to his mother for the first time. I can't help but smile and be extremely happy.

"This is Dani. I'm bringing her to meet our son for the first time." I look down at Dani and smile at the look of awe on her face when she looks at our son. She can't seem to look away. Leaning down, I kiss the top of her head.

I reach out and take our son from the nurse and bring him over to Dani. "Hey, little guy. Look who came to see you," I say as I kneel down next to her, holding our son up so she can see him.

She smiles a teary smile. "Hey, buddy," she says, then reaches out to hold onto his little hand. He latches right on and I can tell he instantly knows who she is just by the sound of her voice.

Handing him over to her, I stand up and watch as mother and son get acquainted with each other.

I stay silent for a while and just watch, awed with seeing Dani with our son. She looked amazing holding our daughter, but she looks even better holding our son. I can't wait to see her with both of them at the same time. But until that day comes, I'll bask in this moment. It's one of the happiest times of my entire life. It's right up there with some of the first moments I spent with Dani, the day I found her again, the day she told me she loved me, and that day at the hospital when we found out we were having a baby.

Finally, Dani looks at me. "Can we name him now?" I can't help but laugh at her question.

"Yeah, Baby Girl, we can." She smiles so big that you'd think I just told her I hung the moon or maybe won the lottery.

"Have you thought of names for him too?" she asks, looking a little unsure. Wanting to see if she's thought about it, I don't tell her that I have thought about it.

"No, have you?"

She's hesitant for a moment, maybe thinking about which names she wants to throw out there.

"Well, I actually only have one name that I thought would be perfect for our boy." When she doesn't say anymore, I take her hand and squeeze it, silently telling her to go on.

"I was thinking we could name him Ezekiel James. We could call him EJ or Zeke for short." I now understand why she was hesitant. It wasn't because she was thinking, it was because she was worried about how I would react to hearing my brother's name.

We haven't talked a lot about Zeke in the past years, not since before I left for college, but what she doesn't know is that I've come to terms with the fact that he's gone. And I've even taken to talking to him, more so recently than before, but still.

I smile at her to reassure her. "I think it's perfect," I say, not needing to say more because it is. It's perfect for our son and exactly what I was thinking of naming him too.

"Really? You don't mind?"

I can't help it. I laugh. "Of course I don't mind. I think it's a great name and that his uncle would be proud his nephew is named after him." She looks at me for a couple of seconds, probably trying to see if I'm telling the truth.

When she sees nothing but happiness and love in my eyes, she finally relaxes a bit and smiles. Then looking down at our son, she says, "Hello, Ezekiel."

He doesn't react like his sister did to her name. Instead, he lets out a loud fart and then you can hear him filling his diaper. Seconds later, the smell hits.

Dani starts laughing so hard it must scare him a little because he starts crying. "Oh, I'm sorry, sweetheart," she says, still with a smile on her face.

The nurse who had him before we came in rushes over and tries to take him from Dani. "Here, let me take him. I'll get him changed and make sure he's taken care of." I don't like her tone or her insinuating that Dani or I can't do it ourselves.

I stand and hold my hand up, stopping her. "No, we've got it." I try to keep the venom out of my voice because I'm sure she's just trying to help, but it still pisses me off.

"I don't mind. I just love taking care of our little guy," the nurse says, still trying to take him out of Dani's arms, but Dani isn't letting go, as she shouldn't. He's *our* son, not this bitch's.

"I said we've got it. Now leave." This time, I let the threat show in my voice, not caring if I sound like a prick.

The nurse stands up straight and looks at me like

I've slapped her and broken her heart at the same time. I give her one last look, then completely ignore her, turning my attention back to Dani. She seems pissed about what the nurse just did too, but she's doing better at keeping a handle on her emotions. Looking at me, she gives me a small smile, then looks around, I assume looking for some diapers.

Remembering where one of the other nurses got some from under his crib, I push past the still-stunned nurse and grab a diaper and some wipes. I pay no attention to the nurse, but if she doesn't step the fuck off soon, I'm going to physically remove her.

"Here you go. After we get him changed, what do you say we take him back to our room, huh?" I ask, just wanting to get out of here and away from that bitch of a nurse. EJ doesn't need to stay up here anymore anyway. Now that Dani is awake, I bet she won't want him away from her for too long.

"Yeah. I like the sound of that," Dani says, looking behind me. I bet the nurse is still standing there. When I turn to see for myself, she must see the hard glare I have because she scurries away. About fucking time, bitch.

I do my best to help Dani change EJ's diaper, but I'm not much help. That's something I'm going to have to learn to do, but I'll get there with Dani's help. She's like a pro already. You'd think she's been changing dirty diapers all her life. That thought makes me laugh and has her looking questionably at me.

"What's so funny?" she asks when I don't say anything.

"Nothing. I was just thinking that you're already a pro at that. But it doesn't surprise me, you're one amazing woman." At my words, she tears up again. It's so unlike Dani to get emotional, but with this pregnancy, it's been a common occurrence. I wonder if once she fully recovers from the births if that will change. I kind of like the way she's been lately. I don't mean this in a mean way, but I think it makes her seem more human. Sometimes, before she was pregnant when things would happen, it was like she didn't feel it or didn't feel it like I thought she should. It was like she was a robot, like she didn't care. Now, though, she shows her emotions so I always know what she's feeling. I don't think I want that to change.

Once EJ is all changed, I take him from Dani and place him in his crib. I make sure we have everything that we need and tell a different nurse that we're taking him down to our room with us and that he won't be back. The doctor already said that he's ready to be released, but since his mother and sister are still here, they've kept him in the nursery to help me out. Now we don't need the help, and if the doctor needs to do anything with EJ, he'll be able to do it all in Dani's room.

It's time that she bond with him and she can't really do that with him in the nursery.

When we walk out the door to leave, I look to the side and see the bitch nurse staring at us. No, she's staring at our son. There's something in her stare that worries me, but knowing that he'll no longer be here and under her care, I brush it off.

CHAPTER 16

Two Weeks Old

Homecoming

Dani

Today is the day my family will finally be whole. Last week, when I was released from the hospital, I was severely depressed. It was so hard leaving my baby at the hospital and going home with Zane and our son. Again, I felt like I had failed my daughter. She was still so small and looked so vulnerable. Even though she's been getting stronger every day, it killed me to leave her.

When we got home last week, Zane stayed by my side twenty-four-seven. He didn't go to the club and didn't work on his new business. Everyone was coming over to see EJ and me, but I just wasn't up for company. Not even when Jax came by to see how I was doing. I hated not having both my babies with me and no one could get my mind off of it.

Zane has been worried and up my ass about every little thing; I need to eat more, I need to bond more with EJ, I need to sleep more, I just need to be *more*. Well, he can just go fuck himself. He has no idea how I'm feeling. I'd like to see him carry what he thought was one baby for eight months, but it turns out it was actually two, pass out from severe pain and blood loss, wake up from a coma four days later, and find out that you delivered two babies. On top of all that, one of them is so small and under-developed she can't come home with you when you're finally released from the hospital. Then try to bond with the baby that is healthy and there with you, while feeling like a failure and horrible mother. Then feel even worse because you're not bonding with the baby you have at home. Yeah, life sucks right now, but today will hopefully make it better. Today, Harley gets to come home. And with her, I hope my normalcy. I don't want to *not* want to be with my son. I love him, but it's just not the same without my daughter.

Walking down the stairs, I see Zane and Mack talking by the door and EJ sleeping in his bassinette in the living room. Heading into the kitchen, I make myself a cup of coffee, then walk over to where Mack and Zane are talking in hushed voices.

"Morning. When are we leaving to go get Harley?" I ask, anxious to get to the hospital. Then I look at Mack. "You staying here with EJ while Zane and I go pick up our girl?" I know it sounds bad, but I would rather not take him with us. I want to be able to give all my attention to my little girl. Plus, EJ doesn't need to be taken places that he's not really needed. He's only two weeks old.

Mack and Zane look at each other before looking back at me. "Actually, Baby Girl, Mack is going to go with me to the hospital to get Harley so you can stay at home with EJ."

I have no idea what to say at first. I'm shocked and a little confused. Why wouldn't I go? Why do I need to stay here with EJ when Mack could just as easily do that? But then I get pissed. How fucking dare he tell me I can't go to pick up my daughter from the hospital?

"Excuse me?" I ask, trying to keep my voice down as to not wake EJ. I may feel like a shitty mother, but I'm *trying* to be good, so that's got to count for something, right?

"Dani, I just think that you should stay here. Rest and spend some time with EJ. You've barely held him since we've been home. With Harley coming home today, you should get all the rest and time in with EJ as you can, because soon we'll have two infants in the house," Zane reasons. And yeah, I can see his point, but I don't want to stay with EJ. I want to go get my daughter.

Then Mack speaks. "Dani, I know you're going through something, and I can even understand it. After everything that happened, you have a right to be all out of sorts. But I think you've had enough time to deal. You are a mother of two, not a mother of *one*. Spend the time with your son and when we get back, you'll have your daughter in your arms." I shake my head, trying to come up with something to get them to understand. I feel like they think I don't like my son. That's not the case, though. I just don't know how to act without my other baby being here too. I feel like

94

she's being cheated or something.

"Plus, one of the nurses is stopping by to make sure your incision is healing all right and that EJ is adjusting well," Zane says, just building more of a case for me to stay here.

"Why can't they just check me out at the hospital?" I ask, though there is no force behind my words, I'm merely speaking now. I'll be staying home with my son while Zane and Mack go to get my daughter.

"Baby Girl, please. Just try to understand. It's easier this way and I really think you need this time with our boy. *Alone*." I do nothing but nod my head. There's no way they'll change their mind so what's the point?

Zane kisses me on the lips and whispers "I love you" before he walks out the door. Next, Mack takes me in his arms and holds me for a few moments. "You're a great mother, Dani, you just need to realize it." He kisses my head and follows Zane out to the truck and they drive away.

I close the door and walk into the living room. Looking into the bassinette at my sleeping baby boy, I try to find it in me to understand and take what they've said to heart, but I can only think about my daughter coming home without her mother there. She'll take her first car ride without me. Wear her first outfit home without me. Walk through the doors to our home for the first time without me. So many firsts that I've already missed, now I'll be missing more.

EJ's cry breaks me out of my thoughts. Looking at him, he's flailing his arms and kicking his legs and screaming. I have no idea what he wants and that scares me to my core. Have I really been so far out of it that I have no idea what my son wants or needs?

Finally understanding what Mack and Zane where saying, I decide right there that I need to be better—for both of my children. They deserve so much more from me.

When I first found out I was pregnant and after the initial shock and fear had passed, I told myself that my son or daughter would have what I never had. They would have a loving mother who would be around as long as possible and a father who would do anything for them. We would never leave them and would always make sure they were loved and cared for.

Now I'm not saying that my life was complete shit because my mother died and my father left, because that's not true at all. I had my grandmother and she was the most amazing, caring woman I ever knew. But I want more for my children.

With new purpose, I pick EJ up and cradle him to my chest. "Shh. It's okay, baby. Mommy's here," I say in a low voice as to not startle him. "I'm so sorry for the way I've acted, but I promise, Mommy will make it right." Walking into the kitchen, I make him a bottle and sit down to feed him. This feels right, for the first time since I came home, this finally feels right. With my baby in my arms and looking into his eyes as I feed him, I finally feel like I can do this.

After he finishes his bottle, I change his diaper and rock him to sleep. Just as I'm laying him down in his bassinette, the doorbell rings. Shit, I almost forgot about the nurse stopping by.

Checking first to make sure EJ didn't wake up, I make my way to the door. Opening it up, I see one of the nurses that was in the nursery with EJ while he was there. "Hello, come in," I say, opening the door wider and motioning her inside.

"Thanks," she says, almost too cheery.

We both walk into the living room and she notices EJ right away, fast asleep. I clear my throat, trying to get her attention so we can get this done. I'd like to change and clean up the house a bit before Zane and Mack get back with Harley.

When she looks at me, she looks pissed that I've interrupted her staring at my son. Well, you can fuck right the hell off. This is *my* house. You're here to check me out and then leave, not ogle my son. "You're here to check my incision, right?" I say, trying to direct this little get-together.

"Yes, of course. Do you have any bandages left over in case when I take your old one off I need to replace it?" I find it odd that she didn't come prepared, but decide to just go get the first-aid kit so she can be done with this and leave.

I make it halfway upstairs, but then realize that I never put it away after Zane changed my bandage yesterday, so it's still in the kitchen. Turning around, I head back downstairs, but when I walk past the living room, I hear something that stops my heart and makes my blood run cold.

"It's okay, my darling boy. Mommy's here now and I won't let that mean old woman near you ever again," the nurse says to EJ while she holds him close to her chest and rocks him back and forth.

CHAPTER 17

Picking Up Harley

Zane

The drive to the hospital is silent. I can't help but think I'm not doing the right thing with Dani. Maybe it wasn't a good idea to leave her alone with EJ when she so clearly didn't want to be there. But how else is she going to bond with our son? She's been so distant since we got home, even while we were still at the hospital now that I think of it. I understand where she's coming from, it about ripped my heart out to leave that day without my little girl too, but that's what she needed at that time. She wasn't strong enough to come home yet, but she is now.

Getting out of the truck, Mack and I walk inside together. "You ready for this?" he asks as we make our way to the elevators.

"More than ready," is all I say, needing to add nothing more. I can't wait to bring Harley home and finally have my family under one roof.

When we make it upstairs, I can see the nurses getting Harley dressed and ready to go for me. They've all become very attached to her and I'm sure they're sad to see her go, but they're all so excited as well. My little girl is ready to start her life at home.

Walking through the doors, I make my way over to the nurses and my daughter without stopping for anything. "How's Daddy's girl today? Are you ready to go home?" I ask, then lean down and kiss her head.

She's gained a lot of weight over the last week so her face is filling out and she doesn't look so small anymore. She's still not as big as her brother, but I know she'll get there.

"She's been a happy little girl today. I think she knew what today was," the nurse says, smiling and laughing.

Once the nurse has her dressed, I take Harley from her. At first, I was so afraid to hold her; she was so small and had all those wires and tubes attached to her. But since they've taken everything off and she's grown a little, I can't put her down. She's definitely Daddy's princess and she's going to be spoiled rotten. They both are.

"I'll go grab the paperwork, then you can be on your way. I know how excited you all must be to take her home, though we're going to miss her." She doesn't wait for me to say anything, not like I was going to anyway, before she walks over to the nurses' station inside the nursery to gather everything we'll need to sign Harley out and take her home.

Mack comes over and runs his hand down the top of her head and her back. "Hello, sweet girl. Papa can't wait for you to come home. We've got a big party planned tonight for you and your brother. All your uncles are excited to meet you." None of my brothers have been able to do anything besides look at her through the glass of the NICU. Only parents, siblings, and grandparents are allowed in so they're chomping at the bit to officially meet her, hold her.

The nurse comes over and has me sign about a hundred papers, then she gathers up some diapers and wipes, puts some formula in the diaper bag, and removes Harley's identification bracelets. "All right. She's all ready to go," the nurse says.

I motion for Mack to bring over the car seat we brought in from the truck and put it on the floor so I can get her strapped in. Fuck, why do they have to make these things so fucking small? Don't they know that it's hard for men to buckle this shit?

Finally getting her strapped in with a little help from the nurse, we are ready to go. "Okay, Harley. Tell all these nice nurses goodbye," I say, walking to the door.

"Bye, sweetie," a few of the nurses say.

We make it almost to the door when I remember what I was going to ask before leaving. Turning around, I speak to the nurse that helped me get Harley together. "I forgot to ask the nurse when she called about the home visit with Dani and EJ today, but could we set up a time with the doctor? Cervical cancer runs in Dani's family, her mother died a few years after having her. I'd like to make sure Dani is in the clear."

The nurse opens her mouth to answer me, but then snaps it shut. She has a look of confusion on her face. "Home visit? We don't do home visits. Dani was supposed to be here this morning, but she didn't show up. We just thought it was because today was a big day, with Harley coming home and all. We can for sure set something up though to get her checked out. When you reschedule her appointment, just mention it," she says. Her words cause ice to run through my veins.

Someone had called me to say they would come to Dani so she wouldn't have to make the trip. Someone who I now know was lying. Fuck, I need to get home! Looking at Mack, I see that he's thinking the same thing I am. Something's wrong.

Handing Harley over to him, I open the door. "Call Toby. Have someone pick you and Harley up and take you to the clubhouse and send Louie to the house. Now!" I don't wait for him to reply, I just run down the hall to the stairs and sprint down to the parking lot. I need to get to Dani and EJ.

***

I stop a block away from the house and see Louie just getting off his bike. "What the fuck is going on? Toby didn't say anything besides Dani was in trouble and to meet you here stat," Louie asks, his face filled with anger and his body tight with tension.

"I got a call that a nurse was stopping by for a home visit, but when I picked Harley up today, they said they don't do home visits. Something's going on, but I have no idea what." We make our way quickly but quietly down the block to my house.

I see a grey car parked on the side of the street in front of our house but I can't tell whose it is. Looking in the window, I see nothing that stands out besides what looks like a brand new infant car seat in the back and the box for it sitting on the floor on the other side.

Motioning for Louie to go around one side of the house, I make my way around the other, ducking low and peeking into the windows as I go along, trying to determine who is inside with Dani and my son, but not seeing anything.

I make it to the back of the house just as Louie is rounding the other side. "See anything?" I ask him in a low voice.

"No, you?" he asks. I shake my head and walk over to the back door. Trying the knob, I thank God that it's not locked. Any other day and I'd be pissed about this fact, but today, I'm grateful.

Quietly pushing the door open, we step inside and listen.

Hearing voices coming from the living room, we quietly make our way through the house, but stop when we hear a struggle and then a gunshot rings out. Not caring anymore about stealth, I break into a run to get to my girl and son.

CHAPTER 18

You Are Not His Mother

Dani

"What are you doing?" I ask, making myself visible to the nurse. I have no idea if I heard her correctly, but the vibe I'm getting now isn't good. And I don't like the way she's holding my son and looking at him like he's her own. Yeah, I definitely heard her right. This bitch is fucking crazy. And a fucking dead woman for coming into my house and trying to take my son away from me. He's mine.

She jumps at the sound of my voice, but turns around to face me, still holding EJ. At first she looks like she's going to try to cover up what I'm pretty sure she said, but then a look of hatred overtakes her face and it's game over. "You fucking heard me, bitch. He's mine and I'm not going to let you have him."

I step forward, not really sure what I'm going to do because she's still holding EJ, I just know I need to get closer to her. I need her to put him down so I can get rid of her—any way I can.

"Okay, look. Why don't you put him down? He's sleeping anyway, and we can talk about this." I try to reason with her, at least until EJ is out of the way and safe, but she's not having any of that.

"You think I'm fucking stupid? As soon as I put him down, you'll come at me, and I can't have that. My son needs me." This girl is delusional. How did she ever get a job at the hospital in the first place? Then I start to wonder if this is the first time she's done this. Oh my God, this is bad. Where the hell is Zane? He should be here by now.

I take another small step forward and hold up my hands in a show of surrender. "I'm not going to do anything, I promise. Let's just talk about this. Maybe we can come up with a solution that's best for everyone, including EJ." Something I said must have been wrong because she turns irate and starts screaming.

"Don't fucking call him that! His name is Timothy, not EJ!" Her yelling wakes EJ up and he starts crying. I don't know what to do! If I try to move closer, there's no telling what she might do. But I can't just sit here while she has my son and he's scared and in danger of being hurt.

"Okay, okay. I understand. Please, just stop yelling. You're scaring him." That makes her stop and look down at him. Then she starts to rock him in her arms.

"Oh, Mommy's sorry, Timothy. I didn't mean to yell. Don't cry."

EJ settles down a little bit, but he's still upset.

Knowing I need to do something fast, I try another route, though she's wary of me so it probably won't work. But I need to try.

"Here," I say, reaching down slowly and grabbing the sling Sara brought over when we came home. "He likes it when you rock him in this." She looks at me hesitantly, then down to the sling. She gets this dreamy look on her face, then she looks at me and smiles.

"Thank you. That's very kind of you," she says, and it's like the last few minutes never happened.

Being cautious and trying to seem like I'm not a threat, I hold the sling out for her to take. I'm hoping she'll lay him down to try and put him in it and then I can make my move, but once she has the sling in her hands, she looks at me in confusion.

"I'm sorry, how much do I owe you again for babysitting?" she asks. What the fuck? This woman is definitely messed up in the head, but this could be the only way to ensure she doesn't freak out again, so I decide to play along. I'll do anything it takes to make sure she doesn't get out of here with my son. I just need to distract her, keep her calm. Then hopefully she'll put him down so I can get to her without hurting him.

"Oh, it was nothing really, so no charge." God this feels so fucking wrong, playing along with her like she's his mother and I'm just a fucking babysitter.

"You don't need to do that! Let me give you some money. Here," she says as she goes to hand EJ over to me, and I can't believe my luck, but then she hesitates. Looking from me, to EJ, then down to the sling. She decides to not give him to me, but it looks like she's going to try and put him in the sling. I can work with that.

"Let me just get him situated, then I can go out and get you some money," she says as she lays EJ on the coffee table, but she is still too close to him. I keep a close eye on her and once I know she's not looking at me, I look around the living room, trying to find something that will help me get her away from him. And then I see it. My purse.

Lying on the table behind the couch is my purse and inside it my gun. I don't want to have to use it with EJ so close, but I'm desperate right now. I can't let her take him out of the house. Stepping slowly and quietly over to it, I keep my eyes on her. She seems to be struggling with the sling, which is good, because it gives me more time.

Once I'm close enough, I reach out and grab my gun, but she sees me move. I put the gun behind my back and act like I'm scratching, but instead place the gun in the waistband of my pants. "What are you doing?" she asks, suspicious now.

Knowing I'm running out of time, I say, "I was grabbing his pacifier for you." She doesn't believe me so I switch tactics.

I take a step forward and hold my hands out. "Here, let me help you." That does the trick. She instantly stands up and holds out her hands to ward me off, but it's too late. She's far enough away that I'm confident I can take care of her and not harm EJ.

Reaching behind me, I pull out my gun and take aim. As soon as she sees what's in my hands, she tries lunging for my son, but it's too late. I pull the trigger and watch her fall to the side, dead. She misses landing on the coffee table where EJ is lying, now crying, by just a few inches, but I had no choice. I had to shoot.

Running over to EJ, I drop the gun and pick him up just as I hear loud footsteps coming from the kitchen into the living room. I don't know how, but I know it's Zane. He's here and everything will be all right.

"Dani!" he shouts when he makes it into the room.

"I'm here," I say, then start to whisper soothing words to EJ, trying to get him to stop crying. "Shhh. You're safe, baby. Mommy has you. I'll never let anyone take you from me. You're safe…you're safe."

Zane rushes over to me and EJ and I see Louie step over to where the nurse is lying on the floor. He's checking to see if she's dead, but he doesn't need to bother. I aimed right at her head, knowing she needed to be stopped. I wasn't going to allow her to do this to anyone else. She's dead.

"Are you both okay? Are you hurt?" Zane asks, panic written all over his face.

Reaching out a hand, I try to reassure him. "We're fine, we're okay."

"I was so fucking scared, Baby Girl. I was just getting ready to leave with Harley when a nurse told me you missed your appointment. I'm so fucking sorry I wasn't here. I'm so fucking sorry," he says, dropping his head into the crook of my neck and he starts to shake. A few seconds later, I feel wetness dampen my shirt. I've only seen Zane cry one time in my life and that was when his brother, Zeke, died. Knowing that he's crying now breaks my heart.

"Hey, we're okay, Zane. We aren't hurt. You got here just in time. It's okay. Everything is going to be just fine." And somehow, I know it will be. Everything is going to be fine, *perfect* even. With Zane, my son and daughter, and everyone at the club by my side, I know that my life is going to be perfect—happy.

I look at Louie, who is watching us, and I give him a reassuring smile. He still hasn't recovered from when he walked into the shop and saw my office with all the blood and thinking the worst happened to me. Then when I was in a coma for four days, it really tore him up. But now, he gives me a smile back. We're going to be okay, all of us.

CHAPTER 19

Meet Your Uncles—All Of Them

Zane

"Zane, I'm fine. EJ is fine. Everyone is expecting us and excited to meet Harley and see EJ. So we're going—with or without you," Dani says as she holds both babies, one in each arm. If I didn't know that my woman and my son were in danger twenty minutes ago and if we didn't just dispose of the nurse that Dani killed, I would be smiling at seeing her with both of our children.

"Baby Girl, you've just been through hell. We almost lost our son, for fuck's sake!" I try to reason.

I can tell she's starting to get pissed off, and not at what she should be right now—what just happened to her and EJ—but at me, when Mack comes up behind me and places his hand on my shoulder. "I think this is exactly what she needs, what we all need, Blaze. Something like this happens and it's always better to be surrounded by those who've got your back. Plus, we've got the bar stocked to celebrate EJ and Harley, but now it looks like we'll be celebrating more than just their birth."

Turning to look at him over my shoulder, I feel myself deflate. Mack is the meanest motherfucker I have seen when he's pissed, and that doesn't happen often, but if he's not freaking out about what just went down, maybe I shouldn't either. He's right, I suppose. We do have more than just the birth of our babies to celebrate tonight. My girl is happy and healthy and she was able to keep her cool when she and our son were in danger. She was able to eliminate the threat without hesitating and without getting herself hurt or putting our son in more danger.

Looking back at Dani, I smile and walk toward her. She's hesitant at first, probably not knowing why I went from being a stone wall to carefree. I take her in my arms, a little awkwardly since she's holding our son and daughter, then kiss the top of her head. "I'm so fucking proud of you, Baby Girl. And not just with how you handled what just happened. When Mack and I left this morning, you were different. Shit, you've been different since we came home without our daughter. But now...fuck, now you're glowing. And the way you look holding both of my children, it makes me love you even more."

I don't usually voice my feelings well or very often, but since nearly losing her four separate times and almost losing both of my kids, I think it's about time I change that.

Dani is still holding our babies between us when I feel her start to shake. Thinking she's laughing at me, I release her and step back, ready to ask what's so funny when I see that she's standing there with her eyes closed and tears rolling down her cheeks. Caught off-guard, I just stand there for a few seconds before I look back at Mack and motion him to grab one of the babies while I grab the other.

"What is it, Dani? Why are you crying?" I ask. She's never really been one to show any type of emotion besides anger and happiness. Aside from when she was pregnant, that is. I've really only ever seen her tears when Zeke and her grandmother died. But since she's been home from the hospital, she hasn't shed one single tear. So why is she crying now?

Once Mack and I have the babies out of her arms, she takes off down the hall and up the stairs. "What the fuck just happened?" I whisper more to myself than to Mack, but he answers anyway.

"She's probably just emotional. She's been through a lot these past few weeks. Just give her a few minutes, she'll be all right."

I pace the floor for what feels like hours with Harley in my arms, but I can't stand waiting here any longer not knowing what is going on with Dani or what she's feeling.

Putting Harley down in the pack-n-play, I don't even bother looking at Mack or telling him where I'm going—he already knows.

When I reach the bathroom upstairs, I hear the faucet running. Knocking softly, I wait for Dani to answer. "Just a minute," she says. I can still hear the tears in her voice, but it's not as bad as I thought it would be.

She opens the door a few seconds later and before

she can even say anything, I take her in my arms. "What was that, Baby Girl? Are you okay?"

She wraps her arms around my back and squeezes me tight. "I'm fine, Zane," she whispers into my chest.

Pulling back a few inches, but still holding her to me, I look down at her and see that her face is a little red and swollen, but the tears are no longer present.

"Why were you crying?"

Looking away, she says, "I don't know. I guess I was ready for you to fight me on going to the club. But then you surprised me by saying what you did. I mean, don't get me wrong, I loved everything you said. It's just I wasn't expecting that, ya know?"

Taken aback, I feel like she's slapped me. Am I that much of an ass or that closed off that me voicing my love to her so openly surprised her so much that she cried?

"Zane, look at me," Dani says, but I just can't. I feel like I've failed her. And by failing her, I'm failing us—our family.

When I don't do as she says and look at her, she steps up to me and grabs my face in both her hands. "Zane. Look at me. You didn't do anything wrong. Sure, you may not have always said those things or are mushy about your feelings, but I know you feel them. I *know* you love me, and Zane, that's all that matters. I don't need you to tell me you love me every five seconds of every day. That's not who you are and it's not who I am." She pauses for a moment and then speaks again. "You just surprised me—in a good way. Those were tears of joy, I can promise you that, babe. But you have to admit, if you were expecting a fight out of me and I turned around and was happy go lucky or something, you would be surprised too. And that's okay. I think it's great that we can still surprise each other."

When she's finished talking, I still don't feel better about what just happened.

"What does it say about me or about our relationship if we're always expecting a fight out of each other, though, Dani? Or the fact that me telling you that I'm proud of you and that I love you is so fucking surprising? Tell me what's so fucking good about that, huh?"

Now I'm starting to get pissed. I fucking love this woman more than my own life and would do anything for her, but what if what we have is unhealthy? What if our love is toxic and no good for the other? Can I live without her in my life? Without her by my side?

"Zane, fighting is what we do—it's who we are. It's not unhealthy, it's just us, and there's nothing wrong with that. Yes, we fight sometimes, but that's all it is. It's a fight. That doesn't mean I love you any less or that you love me any less. Fighting is passion, Zane, and passion is love. So if you're asking me if I'd rather have a passionless relationship, then the answer is no. I would live through everything that has happened in my life—my grandmother dying, knowing my father didn't want me, and getting raped—I would do it all again if I knew that it led me to you, to what we have right now. I love you, Zane Hendricks. I'll love you 'til the day I fucking die."

Hearing her say that she'd go through all that shit again just to be with me has me pissed, but I get it.

Hearing her tell me she loves me is all I needed to

know. Grabbing her face in my hands, I look her in the eyes. "I fucking love you too, Baby Girl. Always," I say, then I take her lips in a rough kiss.

A few minutes later, we break apart, breathless. "We should probably get going or the guys are going to get worried," she says wistfully.

I kiss her once more, but this time softly before I take her hand a lead her downstairs.

***

Pulling into the parking lot of the clubhouse, I feel almost nervous, though I can't pinpoint why. I do have a surprise for Dani, but that's not it. There's nothing to be nervous about. We're introducing our son and daughter to my brothers tonight—their uncles—but I still feel like this is a big deal. It *is* a big deal, all of it.

"Are you nervous?" I ask Dani, who is sitting in the truck beside me, not moving.

Turning toward me, she smiles. "Yes, but not about them meeting their niece and nephew. More about what we're about to walk into," she says with a laugh.

Not really following, I look at her and wait for her to elaborate.

"Before we left, Mack told me that the guys put this party together. Said they even went as far as cleaning and decorating. I'm afraid to think of what they used for decorations—colored condoms and sex toys hanging from the ceiling?"

Picturing what she just said has me grimacing at first, but then laughing so hard that my stomach hurts before I get serious again. "Fuck, Baby Girl, you don't think they'd really do that, do you?" I ask. Maybe I should just turn around and head home. It can't be sanitary to bring two newborn babies in there knowing what goes down inside when the boys let loose.

I'm almost ready to turn the truck back on and head back home when Dani laughs and gets out of the truck. "Zane, it's fine. No, I don't think they would really do that, it was just funny to think about. Let's go. I can't wait to show our babies off to everyone."

She shuts her door, only to open the back door behind her to get EJ out of his car seat. Following her lead, I do the same and get Harley out of hers.

When I meet her in front of the truck, she holds out her free arm, silently asking me to give her our daughter so she can hold both babies. Even though I want to hold Harley, I know she needs this more than I do. She missed so much already, so I can give this to her.

I follow her into the clubhouse and once we're inside, I stop and stare at all my brothers. They're are all dressed nice, and looking around the room, I see a huge banner hanging over the bar that says, "Welcome home, EJ and Harley." Blue and pink streamers hang haphazardly around the room, and blue and pink balloons are taped to different surfaces; walls, bar stools, the bar, pool table, even on the stripper pole.

Looking toward Dani, I see her face light up like the Fourth of July. She's smiling at our family and introducing them to our son and daughter. She looks so happy and carefree. Looking at her now, I know that I'll spend the rest of my life trying to make her look and feel like she does right now.

Seeing Jaxon sitting in a dark corner, I head his way.

"You ready to reveal the surprise?" I ask, anxious to see Dani's reaction.

When Jaxon came into town, I was pissed and leery of him, but now...I'd trust him with my life. But more importantly, I'd trust him with Dani's and my kids' lives.

After all the shit went down with that nurse, Jaxon got real angry. Said he felt helpless. That something could have happened to EJ and Dani, and he wouldn't have been able to do a single thing to help. I never expected him to come at me with his proposal of joining the club, but frankly, I'm glad he did. He'll make a great brother.

"Hell yes, I'm ready," he replies.

Slapping his shoulder, I pinpoint where Dani is standing by the bar talking to Sara and Toby, who are each holding one of the babies, then make my way toward her with Jaxon trailing behind me.

"Baby Girl, I've got something to tell you," I say in a voice void of all emotion. I don't want to give anything away.

Turning around to face me, she looks at me questioningly. "Oh yeah?"

"Yeah. Well, actually, it's more like I wanted to *show* you." I step to the side so she has a clear line of sight to Jaxon.

As soon as she sees him, she knows what it is I wanted to show her. Jaxon is wearing a cut with a Prospect patch on it clear as day. Gasping, she looks between me and Jaxon before hurling herself into his arms.

"Oh my God! Are you for real right now? You better not be playing a sick joke on me or so help me, I will kick your ass; right here, right now," the excitement clear in her voice.

"It's for real, Dani girl. As of this morning, I'm officially a Forsaken Sinners Prospect."

I only have a slight need to rip her away from him as she jumps into his arms, but I know she needs this right now. She was so happy when Jaxon came back into her life and even more so when he decided to stay. I'm just happy I was able to play a part in keeping him here for her. It's just icing on the cake that I got a new employee out of it and now a soon-to-be brother.

CHAPTER 20

First Birthday

Zane

A year ago today was the scariest and happiest day of my life; it was the day I almost lost Dani, but it was also the day my son and daughter were born. I thank God every day that He saved all three of them.

Then the day I brought Harley home, I thought I was going to lose her again. Walking into the house and hearing that gunshot, I thought that was it. But when I saw her and our son safe, I broke down. I've only cried twice in my life: the day my brother died and the day I thought I lost Dani again, and our son. But once again, Dani proved that she can protect herself and that she would do anything to protect her children.

Things are perfect now. The kids are healthy, the club is running smoothly and with no problems from rivals, and Dani got a clean bill of health from the doctor. When she was finally able to re-schedule her missed appointment from when that nurse tried to take EJ from us, they found cancer cells on her cervix. I was devastated and pissed off at the world. But then they did a biopsy to see if it was cervical cancer, and the results came back great. She'll get checked more often, but as of today, she's cancer free. I still freak out and worry that I'm going to lose her, but I'm trying to get better. I guess I'll always be an "overprotective caveman," has Dani puts it. She's just going to have to get over it.

I know I drive her crazy, but I need her and the kids to be safe. I know that if something were to happen to even one of them, it would destroy me. She's just going to have to live with it, and the kids too. I'm sure when they get older, I'm going to drive them insane, especially my daughter. I've come a long way, but I'll always be protective of my Dani and the kids. More so with Dani and Harley, though. It's going to drive them all crazy.

I can tell EJ is going to be a lot like me—a protector. He's so aware of his sister, it's astonishing that he's only one, but when people come near her that he's never seen before, he finds a way to get to her. It's amazing really, but it makes me glad knowing that not only will his sister have me and my brothers to protect her, but she'll have her brother too.

And Harley, she's still smaller than her brother, but she has exceeded what the doctors thought possible. She was able to put on the weight and keep it on very quickly and she never had any health problems that you sometimes hear babies have if they're born prematurely. She even took her first step before her brother did.

Both of the kids have me and their mama wrapped around their little fingers, but Dani has a soft spot for EJ and I guess you could say I have one for Harley. Dani always makes fun of me, telling me I'm turning soft because I'll give my little princess anything she wants, especially when she starts crying. It just breaks my heart. Dani's the same way with our son, though she just doesn't see it like I do. But hey, isn't that the way it's supposed to go—Mama's boy and Daddy's girl?

Today, we're having a big party for their birthday at the clubhouse. All my brothers will be there and I'm sure there are going to be tons of gifts for the kids. Harley and EJ have more than any one-year-old could ever need or ever possibly want. Yeah, my kids are spoiled as fuck. But I can't put all the blame on my brothers, I'm just as guilty. Dani is always making fun of me and saying I spoil them, but I couldn't care less. I want my kids to have everything they could ever dream of.

"Zane! Do you have the kids' bags packed and in the truck?" Dani yells from upstairs.

"Yes I do. Everything is ready to go. We're just waiting on you," I yell back, then look down at the kids playing with blocks on the floor. "Your mother is going to make us late for your party since she just had to go in to work this morning for some reason."

EJ stands and makes his way toward me. I pick him up and walk to the bottom of the stairs. "Mama. Mama!" he says, and I know that hearing him, Dani will move faster so she doesn't upset him. See, Mama's boy.

"All right, all right, I'm ready. Let's go," she says,

bounding down the stairs. When I see her, my breath catches in my throat and I have to adjust my cock inside my pants. Holy fuck, she looks hot! She's wearing tight black leather pants, a tight white tank top, and her favorite leather jacket. My woman is a fucking MILF.

When she walks past me, I slap her ass hard. "You trying to drive me insane, Baby Girl?" I groan.

"Is it working?" she asks, then winks before heading toward the kitchen.

Growling in frustration, I say, "You're going to kill me one of these days." That makes her laugh, then she turns around and comes back toward me and places a heated kiss on my lips.

"Mack's watching the kids tonight. And when we get home, I've got a surprise for you."

When she walks away this time, she puts a little extra sway in her hips. "You better watch it, Baby Girl, or else you might find yourself in a compromising position," I say just loud enough for her to hear. Her laugh rings loudly from the kitchen, but I let her be. I'll have my cock buried deep in her pussy soon enough.

***

After I pull into the clubhouse parking lot, Dani goes to get EJ out of the truck and I get Harley out. As soon as their little feet touch the ground, they're off, running as fast as they can to the front door where Mack is waiting for them with a balloon in each hand.

"Papa!" they both yell at the same time. Yeah, they have Mack wrapped around their fingers too. It's sometimes funny to watch such a big hard ass like Mack be so soft and calm with them, but it's a good look on him. I hope he can find someone and settle down. He's not old, but he's getting to that age that I just want him to be happy and my hope is having an Old Lady would do that for him.

Taking Dani's hand, I walk with her up to Mack. She gives him a hug and whispers something to him before he looks at me and smiles. Reaching out to shake my hand, he says, "I can't believe they are a year old already."

"I know. They're getting so big, they need to stop growing!" Dani says with a laugh, but I can hear a little bit of sadness hidden behind her words.

Mack leans down, picks up both kids, then turns and takes the kids into the backyard. Dani follows, but as soon as we pass a storage closet, I can't wait anymore.

Grabbing her by the wrist, I open the door and yank her in behind me. Locking the door, I flip on the switch and look at her with my intent clearly written all over my face.

"Zane, we can't! It's the kids' birthday party!" She tries to stop me, but I'm too far gone. Seeing her look the way she looks today is just too much for me to handle. I can't wait until we get home. I'll fuck her here, right now to take the edge off and then when we get home, I'll take my time with her.

"Can't wait, Baby Girl. I need to be inside you," I say before I take her lips in a hard kiss.

Reaching down, I unbutton her pants and slip my hand inside. She gasps when I flick her clit, but I swallow it with my mouth and continue working her hard and fast. With my other hand, I pull down the top of her shirt so I can suck on her beautiful tits, but I stop when I see a bandage over her left breast. "What the fuck is that?" I growl.

Dani must know exactly what I'm talking about because she looks down before she brings her gaze back to mine. She smiles and then starts to take the gauze off. I have no idea what it could be, but it has me worried.

"I was going to wait till tonight to show you, but I guess now's a good time too," she says just as the gauze pulls free and I'm left looking at a new tattoo over her heart. It's the MC's emblem and name, but what it says below it makes my breath catch and my cock harder than I think it's ever been.

"I've thought about it a lot lately, and I know I said I would never do it, but I changed my mind. I love you more than my own life, Zane, and I love this club. It's time I show that love and loyalty to everything that sees it," she says, looking at me with a smile on her face, but I can't stop looking at the brand that marks her. *My* brand. At the bottom of the FSMC emblem, it reads "Property of Blaze."

Not able to hold out any longer, I pull her pants down roughly, then turn her around before bending her over. "Do you have any idea what it does to me to see my mark on you?" I growl as I reach down to release my hard cock. "Hold on tight, Baby Girl, I can't wait any longer." I ram into her tight, wet pussy in one thrust. "Fuck!"

I don't give her time to adjust, I just keep pounding into her with a hard, fast rhythm. "Oh God, Zane, right there." She moans, and I can feel her pussy quiver around my cock. She's close.

"Don't come until I tell you to," I demand, needing her to wait until I'm ready. I want to feel her grip my cock as we both come.

Grabbing her hips roughly, I pick up the pace, racing toward the finish line. "Fuck, Baby Girl. I love the way your pussy feels on my cock." At my words, her pussy starts to contract and I know she can't hold off any longer. "Come, Dani. Come all over my cock," I growl into her ear as I lean over her and thrust into her three more times.

"Yes!" she screams and I feel her come hard.

"Shit. Fuck!" I still inside of her as I feel her pussy milk my cock.

We stay like that for a few minutes, both of us trying to catch her breath. When I finally pull out, she whimpers at the loss. "Come on, Baby Girl. Let's celebrate our kids' birthday. Then tonight, I'm going to fuck you nice and slow, all night long."

CHAPTER 21

The Birthday Party

Dani

The party is in full force when Zane and I finally come outside. We should have been out here sooner, but I can't complain, I needed that quickie just as much as he did. Plus, I'm kind of glad I was able to show Zane my new tattoo. I honestly didn't think I could hold that in any longer.

When I asked Mack to meet me at the shop this morning, he thought I wanted to talk him about the shop and how things are going with the kids and work. But when he got there, I got right down to the real reason I asked him to come. I've thought about this long and hard since that night when we had a heart to heart in the bathroom. I didn't lie when I told him I would re-live every bad thing that happened to me as long as I got him in the end. I know he doubts me—us—sometimes, but I'm hoping that with this new tattoo—*his brand*—that he'll finally understand

and believe in my love for him.

Sara catches my eye and I make my way over to her as Zane crosses to where the kids are playing with Mack and a few of the brothers. "Hey! I've been looking for you!" she says, though I'm sure she knows exactly what Zane and I were up to.

"Yeah, sorry. Something came up that I had to take care of," I say with a wink. Yeah, she knows.

"I bet." She laughs and then pulls me over to a picnic table. "So, I wanted to talk to you about something. Toby and I have set a date for the wedding. Now, it's not going to be anything big or fancy, but I'd love it if you would be my Maid of Honor." I'm stunned. Toby and Sara got engaged right after all that shit went down with her crazy ex, but up until now, they never made any mention about setting a date. When they first told us they were getting married, they just said it would happen when the time was right, but I think their reason for waiting was because of my pregnancy and things being a little tense in the club. I don't know what's going on, but something seems to be brewing. But I'm secretly glad they've waited.

"Oh my God, of course! I'd love to me your Maid of Honor! Thank you!" I say then pull her in for a hug. Sara has become like a sister to me. I knew when Toby first told me about her, even before I met her, that we would be close. I never had any siblings, but to me, she is my sister.

Sara looks happy and a little relieved. "Thank you! I was a little worried that you wouldn't want to," she says hesitantly.

"Why on Earth would I *not* want to? This is the

biggest day of your life. You both mean the world to me. Of course I will stand beside you while you marry the man of your dreams. I'm honored, Sara." I'm humbled that she thought of me.

Toby is like a brother to me, more so than any of the other men here, even Louie. When I first met him, I felt a connection to him and it's always been there. He's been there for me, he's helped me grow into the woman I am today, and he's protected me and helped make sure I could protect myself and those I love. I couldn't be happier for both of them. They're perfect for each other and destined to be together. I just know it.

Sara pulls me into another hug. "Thank you. You have no idea what it means to me." I just nod, afraid if I say anymore, that either or both of us will break down into tears, and today is not a day I want to cry – whether they are happy tears or not.

"Mama!" I hear EJ yell from across the yard. I smile at Sara and stand up.

"Duty calls," I say, then make my way over to my baby boy.

"Mama!" EJ says again just as I make it over to him.

"Yes, baby, I'm right here." I bend down and pick him up, holding him close to my chest. God I love this little boy. He looks just like his daddy and I couldn't be happier about that.

"Mama!" he yells and wiggles in my arms, waving his arms around and toward the presents. Of course. I should have known as soon as we got here that we wouldn't make it long before one or both of the kids would see the presents and want to rip into them.

"Not yet, baby boy. We need to wait a little while longer," I say, hoping I can distract him or talk him into waiting, but no such luck. Harley comes wobbling up to me and pulls at my leg. Picking her up, it's a struggle at first with EJ squirming around, but I finally get her into my other arm.

"Mum mum mum," she says.

Knowing there's no way they'll wait, I place a kiss on both of their cheeks before letting them down. "Okay, okay. Let's go find your father and we'll open presents." I set them both down and they both take off as fast as their little wobbly feet can go, searching for their father.

They find him almost instantly, and run and jump into his lap as he sits and talks with Toby, Louie, and Jax. Watching him laugh and smile as they squeal and yell in delight about opening up presents, I realize how good my life turned out. I thought destiny was just using me as a toy and liked to see how far she could throw me before I'd break. I hated the shit that was thrown my way in my life and thought it was to punish me or break me down. But now, I see it for what it was. It was a way to make me stronger, to build me up, and make me the person I am today. To lead me where I am today, where I belong. Here with my family and friends, the love of my life, and my two beautiful children. I still can't believe I have everything I ever wanted, and more.

Now I realize that sometimes, destiny isn't made, it's born.

ACKNOWLEDGEMENTS

I want to thank my family the most. You all have stood beside me through this whole endeavor of me trying to fulfill my dream of being an author. Whether it's just been encouraging words, brainstorming with me about characters, scenes, and whatever else. Thank you all so much.

I also want to thank my girl, Elaine, for taking a chance on a new author and for sticking beside me. You've helped me pimp, got the word out about me and my books, and you've been an amazing friend. Whoever said that you can't make lifelong friendships on Facebook doesn't know shit. I appreciate all that you've done to help me with my books, but most of all, I appreciate your friendship. I love you, girl!

And of course, I can't say this enough, but thank you to all my readers. I never expected such a huge following, but I'm thrilled that you have stuck beside me through everything. I wouldn't have gone this far without you, and neither would my characters. Thank you all so much! <3 <3 <3

ABOUT THE AUTHOR

I grew up in a small town in Iowa. I have 2 older sisters and amazing parents. Growing up, I was always a daddy's girl, hanging out with him in the garage, fishing, and building stuff. I loved to play softball and swimming, but reading, telling stories, and writing were my passion, even at a young age. I took a break from writing for a while, but you could always find me with a book in my hand.

I have three children–two boys and a girl. They are my whole world. Even when I'm having the worst day ever, they brighten up my day and make me smile.

A few years ago, there was this story that would always play out in my head and no matter how many times I went through it, from beginning to end, it would never fade. So I decided to put it on paper. I didn't plan on publishing it, but when it was almost done, a friend asked to read it. She said it was a story that needed to be shared. And that's what started my writing career.

I love all genres of books, and even though I started with writing MC Romance, I have a whole book of ideas, so you can expect more from me than just MC, though romance is in my blood.

Even though I currently work two jobs, my ultimate dream is to become a full time author. I want to be able to spend my days filling pages with stories. I want to be the reason people find a reason to smile or laugh from lines on a page. Reading a book allows me to live in someone else's shoes, even if only for a few minutes. It's a way to leave my life and troubles behind and I want to be help others do that as well.

Facebook:
https://www.facebook.com/pages/Author-Shelly-Morgan/809266812448318

Twitter:
https://twitter.com/Shelly_Morgan34

Website:
https://www.goodreads.com/author/show/10914599.Shelly_Morgan

Join my fan group on Facebook:
https://www.facebook.com/groups/866725876706109/

Don't forget…
If you haven't already, check out the first two books in the Forsaken Sinners MC Series.

Rewriting Destiny – Dani and Zane's story and prequel to the series

Fighting Destiny – Toby and Sara's story

Coming soon…

Defying Destiny – Louie's story

Owning Destiny – Mack's story